THE VISITOR

A Story of Suspense

THE

VISITOR

by Josephine Poole

HARPER & ROW, PUBLISHERS, INC.
New York, Evanston, San Francisco, London

THE VISITOR

 Printed in the United States of America. For information address Harper & Row, Publishers, Inc., 10 East 53rd Street, New York, N.Y. 10022.

Library of Congress Catalog Card Number: 72-80367
Trade Standard Book Number: 06-024768-1
Harpercrest Standard Book Number: 06-024769-X

FIRST EDITION

To Pelo and David

with love

What is that bell ringing for?
said Meet-on-the-road.

To ring bad spirits home again,
said Child-as-it-stood.

OLD ENGLISH BALLAD

THE VISITOR

1

The country with its wide and empty horizons repeated the desolation of the sea. Cormundy Hill, ten miles inland, had the look of a buoy or lighthouse.

St. Augustine was supposed to have rested there, and his church crowned the hill. Its skyey spire had a circling choir of gulls. During the Reformation, cattle had been stalled in the nave, but they had worn the floor to a devotional unevenness like the entrance to a shrine. Four ancient figures, angels or evangelists, still held up the corners of the carved roof, and on fine afternoons a heavenly rose window dappled the modern altar with reflected glory. There was no resident vicar at present; matins were said at St. Augustine's on the first Sunday in the month.

Cormundy Village took the gradient of the hill with

funny cramped houses, steep terraces, and unexpected flights of steps. All around stretched miles of corn. Some trees had been left as windbreaks; there were no hedges. In spring the village floated like an island in a jade-green, deepening tide. In summer the combines were brought in, grinding between the properties, as wide as the road but sounding like insects from the hill with their hot-weather drone. They were more efficient than human labor, so men were out of work in Cormundy, though it had been a rich village in the old days.

After harvest the stubble was fired. It went off like a cavalry charge, speeding and thundering. In sunlight the flames were insignificant, a gobbling frill to the clouds of hot brown smoke; but as soon as it was dark they sprang in flickering plots around the beleaguered village where everything was dusted with burnt chaff. Then in autumn the east wind tore across with its knives and scourges. There was no hope left in the savaged fields. The iron hooves of the wind struck up eddies of yellow leaves and husks.

It had been such a bitter day when Mr. Bogle arrived in Cormundy, by bus from the nearest town. The advent of this bus was a daily occurrence, at ten to six; and as it stopped opposite the Nag's Head, it was a topic of conversation among the men waiting for the bar to open. Mr. Bogle was the only person to alight, but even in a crowd he would have attracted attention.

First he dangled one very long leg and black shoe out of the bus, seeking the ground. The second leg followed, and by degrees the whole of him, cautiously. He was a tall man, and stooped. His hands were pulled down to the level of his knees by the weight of the suitcases he was carrying, while under one arm he gripped a violin. He had a blot of a nose, a wide mouth, and a turnipy kind of tufty hair at the back of his lumpy head. His body was the shape of a fly's. He wore a flapping black suit with a week's mail bulging out of the pockets, thick spectacles, and no hat. He was still pulling himself together on the pavement when the bus, having waited in vain for passengers, started downhill toward the darkening fields.

Mr. Bogle crossed the road to speak to the loitering men, but at that moment the Nag's Head opened and they began pushing inside. However, he caught up with someone at the back to ask the way. He had a scrap of paper with an address written on it. The man he had chosen to help him looked at it impatiently.

"You got off too soon," he said. "If you had stayed on, it would have taken you past the gate." And they both glanced over the surrounding country, where in the distance the traveling bus could still be traced, like glittering jewelry being drawn away. "Take that road, you can't miss it. It's the only wood round here." And he hurried after his mates.

The road was steep at first. Mr. Bogle had a lurching, headlong gait, toppling downhill. Now the wind had dropped, the darkening sky pressed softly like the breast of a nesting bird over the land, though there were clear streaks in the west where the sun had fallen. The waiting fields rose to meet him with every step he took, but he gave no sign that he saw anything other than the road which he followed for twenty minutes or so. Behind his back the lighted village twinkled on the hill.

He reached the wood. There was no gate, but pillars showed where it had hung. On top of them, facing each other, a pair of stone beasts reared with shields, worn to a smooth anonymity. An unpaved drive wound between the trees, and Mr. Bogle turned into it; it was soft underfoot with a mixture of earth and rotten leaves. He seemed a hybrid animal himself as he loped along, his black shape passing rapidly from trunk to trunk. High above his head the stripped branches made a jigsaw of the dusky sky, like leads in a window.

In front of him a house began to form, a darkness glimpsed through the wood. As he emerged at last with a free view of it, a colony of rooks flapped upward, cawing and falling again behind the old roofs. And a black horse that had been grazing along the fringe of trees lifted its head and stared at the stranger. But after a moment it bent to pull at the grass, the knotted reins falling forward to its ears, a buckle or stirrup iron glinting now and then as it moved.

Mr. Bogle surveyed the L-shaped building with its halo of protesting birds. Patched with ivy, stained with age and damp, it had in the dusk a very derelict appearance. Two of the windows were lit, however, on the ground and first floors, and he plunged across the drive. The single door was set against the angle of the house. He tugged at the iron bellpull. A varnished board bore the name FURY WOOD burned into its grain.

Mr. Bogle was doubtful whether the bell worked. He bent toward the door, listening, the suitcases he was holding nearly touching the ground.

"Are you sure he's coming today?" Harry Longshaw asked. He was lying down in his bedroom, drawing a white fantail pigeon from life; it was posing obligingly on the rail across the foot of the bed. Most of the time it seemed to be asleep, but occasionally it rolled one brown eye in Harry's direction, as if to inquire how its portrait was progressing.

His sister Margaret peered at a scrawled letter she had put for reference behind the clock on the mantelpiece.

"I think so. Doesn't that look like October 23rd to you?" she asked the third person in the room, Rupert Musgrave, to whom she was engaged to be married.

"Could be," he agreed. "I thought he was meant to tutor Harry. His writing is practically illegible."

"I expect it means he's clever," said Margaret optimistically. "Like doctors."

"With any luck he won't turn up till tomorrow," Harry remarked, shading in feathers.

They heard the bus pass the gate without stopping.

"I'm going to make tea," said Margaret. "I'm sick of waiting. I've been expecting him all day."

"Chuck me a biscuit for the bird," said Harry, shoving his paper and pencils under the pillow.

"For it to eat off the blanket? No thanks! It took me ages to clean your room this morning," his sister answered decidedly.

"Come on, Maggie, it isn't like you to fuss! He's earned a treat, poor bird." She gave in, as he knew she would; as she invariably had since the illness which had crippled him a year ago.

There was nothing stylish about Harry's room. The carpet was threadbare, and the slipcovers were too loose for the three armchairs which had sagged and shrunk like old people. The faded curtains looked like ruined maps. There were plenty of books, clothbound editions as well as paperbacks. On a dresser stood photographs of Mr. and Mrs. Longshaw, who were dead.

All the family portraits had been hung for their health in Harry's room, since it was the warmest in the house. They crowded the walls, shoulder to shoulder, gay, grim, plain or handsome, posed for social or naval engagements. The ladies showed off the fashions in dresses and dogs; the men paraded a century of uniforms. The youngest, a boy of Harry's age, was standing by a broken column in the act of unrolling a parchment on which the family motto was inscribed in careful copperplate. The pictures came to an end with him, and so had the family fortune.

Harry had never taken much notice of his ancestors before he was ill. Now they were old friends, reassuring with their swords and cannon and telescopes, their heritage of bravery and hope.

Margaret balanced the kettle on the logs in the grate. On the mantelpiece, beside the clock, a loaf of bread and package of butter waited to be made into toast. She had arranged a tea tray on a low table before the fire. She was eighteen, three years older than Harry, though at first glance they might have been twins. They both had tawny wavy hair and gray eyes, and he was easily as tall as she was. There was a warm informality about Margaret that people found very attractive. It was altogether lacking in her brother. He had the sort of awareness that creates wariness; he would be truthful before he was kind.

Rupert already behaved like one of the family. He was sitting near the fire in a deep armchair, the heel of one shoe balanced on the toe of the other, his lively blue eyes often resting on Margaret. He introduced an unexpected note of richness and assurance; from his golden hair to his stitched leather soles it was obvious that he was a very eligible young man. They planned to be married on Christmas Eve. The house was already up for sale; Harry was going to live with them on Rupert's farm, on the farther side of Cormundy.

Harry lifted the pigeon and stood it to roost in a corner cupboard overhanging his bed.

"What other creatures have you got in there?" Rupert demanded, sniffing suspiciously.

"Mice. I let the jackdaw go."

Rupert appealed to Margaret. "Must he bring his menagerie with him to the farm?"

"One day you'll be glad you fostered my youthful inclinations," Harry observed, settling down with a book.

"Have a cup of tea," said Margaret, the peacemaker. She crouched on the hearthrug to make toast.

"What have mice and jackdaws to do with marine biology?" asked Rupert, exasperated.

Harry did not know the answer to that, so he kept quiet. Margaret said, "I don't think Mr. Bogle's coming." But at that moment, as though the expected visitor had been following the conversation, the bell rang.

"There he is, damn him!" said Harry.

Rupert got up. "I'll let him in."

Mr. Bogle heard a light tread across the hall. He mounted the step, his mouth stretched in an attentive grin.

Rupert opened the door. "Mr. Bogle!" He sounded surprised, even taken aback to find the name fitted the person so exactly; but quickly remembered his manners.

"Come in. We're already acquainted through our letters. It's nice to meet you at last!"

The slam of the door echoed through the tiled hall. The electric light bulb hanging from the ceiling moved in the draft, rocking the balance of light and shadow.

"You'll be staying till Christmas," said Rupert. "Is that all your luggage?"

"Oh, I'm a light traveler," said Mr. Bogle.

They went upstairs. The hall pierced the height of the house up to a dirty glass cupola which leaked when it rained. The best bedrooms lay off a landing; Rupert pushed open a door and switched on the light. "Here you are. We've done our best to make you comfortable." Mr. Bogle stood on the threshold, looking in. Rupert said, "Perhaps you'd like to put down your suitcases, and your—" he hesitated, "—your instrument."

Mr. Bogle set them down side by side, with a glance round his new abode. It was a big, square room. The wallpaper had a design of Imperial statues, draped and commanding, realistic in the artificial light. There was a large desk, and shelves for books, and the old-fashioned, canopied bed had a clean cover. Margaret had put a vase of chrysanthemums on the bedside table.

"Now you must meet the others," said Rupert, leading the way down a passage. Mr. Bogle brushed both walls with his hands as he followed. His dry fingers made a scraping sound against the plaster.

The passage branched right and left along the east wing of the house. They turned left, still marching one behind the other—it was too narrow to do anything else. At the far end, in Harry's room, Margaret got up quickly to smooth her hair in front of the glass over the fireplace. She met her brother's eyes in it, and gave his reflection an encouraging smile.

The door opened. Rupert stepped aside, and there loomed the tutor, filling the space. When he moved forward Margaret was touched by his stoop and ingratiating manner.

"You must have had an awful journey," she said. "Come and sit down by the fire. I'll pour you some tea. We usually have our meal at five, because it suits Harry better. But I can get you some supper."

Mr. Bogle assured her that he had already eaten. He lowered himself into an armchair, stretching his legs until his heels rested on the fender. He took three spoonfuls of sugar in his tea, and as many minutes to stir them in; he made a keen survey of the room as he stirred and stirred. When he had finished with the pictures one by one, he rested his eyes on Harry. And Harry was conscious of the scrutiny, though he went on reading.

"This is a cozy room," said Mr. Bogle, supping tea. "This is a real treat for an old bachelor like me. Oh, I shall be happy here, I know! We'll get on splendidly together."

"I'm afraid the rest of the house isn't very comfortable," said Margaret, smiling. "You must tell me if you're cold. There are plenty of hot-water bottles, and extra heaters if you need them."

"Oh, the cold won't worry me! I've never been sensitive to extremes of temperature. I remember when I was in the South Seas people used to complain of the heat, but I can't say I noticed it much. It's all to do with the pores of the skin. I never sweat; now that's odd, isn't it?"

"What were you up to in the South Seas?" asked Rupert.

"Collecting material," said Mr. Bogle, with a clumsy wave of the hand. "Old customs, old dances, old beliefs—anything of that sort. They were fruitful years. Some of those islands make Stonehenge look like a bowling alley."

Harry risked an ironical glance at Margaret, and caught the tutor's eye. A very dark and knowing eye it was. He blushed, and bent over his book.

"Harry used to collect fossils," said Margaret. "Once he dug up a Roman coin in the wood."

"It was half-a-crown when I got the muck off it," he said, without looking up.

There was a silence, broken by Rupert who had been taught the social graces.

"Talking of the wood, why *Fury* Wood? I've often wondered whether it dates back to the Vikings. Maybe they raided here, before St. Augustine. Or would it have been after? I ought to join you for history lessons,

Harry," he said, shaking his head. "I can't sort out anything earlier than the Tudors."

"Fury means ferret," said Harry. "The word ferret comes from the French *furet.* Those are stone ferrets on the pillars at the drive end." His legs had begun to ache, as they often did in the evening. If he complained, Margaret and Rupert would be anxious; sometimes he hated their loving eyes. He stealthily sought a more bearable position on the creaking mattress.

"Oho!" exclaimed Mr. Bogle, kicking up one foot. "A budding scholar I see! But Fury might mean *fiery,* don't you think? The original wood was burnt—you knew that, of course."

"No," said Margaret. "I never heard that before."

"I'm talking of—what? Three or four hundred years ago. Rather before your time," said Mr. Bogle, including the ancestors in a slight bow. He took another piece of toast, dipping it into his tea before he bit it up in wide mouthfuls. The rim of his cup had a scum of melted butter.

"Oh yes," he went on with his mouth full. "The trees were cut down and burnt, and the spring filled in; that was the usual procedure when they were mopping up witchcraft. All the same it was rash to build on the site. I noticed you have a pump outside; water always returns sooner or later. But if you didn't know about the fire, what sense did you make of *that*?" and he jabbed with his forefinger at the mantelpiece.

Under the shelf where the clock ticked, and half a

loaf remained in a litter of crumbs, an ancient beam covered the width of the chimney. At some point in history a Latin sentence had been scratched into it, with a nail perhaps. One needed to peer at it to read it, though Harry and Margaret knew it by heart. But it was Mr. Bogle who quoted it now, showing off his knowledge of Latin with an English translation: " 'Arise, thou avenger to come, out of my ashes.' It's Virgil, of course."

His companions were gaping at him.

"You've been here before!" Margaret exclaimed.

"No, indeed. I've never been to this house. But I've wanted to come here for years. Oh, I was delighted when you answered my advertisement! A carving, like this one; a superstition; an old tune; these are the clues that put me on the scent." He looked from Margaret to Rupert and Harry. Their blank faces seemed to amuse him; his grin spread until it nearly joined his ears. "But I'm a witch-hunter!" he burst out, giving the game away.

Margaret was taken aback by this unexpected craze. "A witch-hunter!" Harry repeated with relish. He had been against the idea of a tutor from the start, and now it pleased him to find that this one was touched in the head. "Then you'll enjoy our covens on Saturday nights. Initiation free, with rites; there are plenty of broomsticks for hire in the cupboard under the stairs."

Mr. Bogle ignored him. "Don't let it worry you," he begged Margaret. "I shan't burst into flames, or disappear in a cloud of smoke, I promise you! It's a hobby, that's all; and where's the harm of delving into these things in an academic way? The truth never hurt anyone!"

"What would you do if you found a witch?" asked Rupert. "It might be a bit disconcerting."

"Not at all," said Harry before Mr. Bogle could answer. "You just remember your magic words, and turn it into a princess or a hundred pounds."

"I have great hopes of Cormundy," said Mr. Bogle. "It used to be a hotbed of witchcraft; I can't believe there's nothing left under the surface. It's such a backwater. The whole ambience of the place, so quiet, almost dead in fact—it's most encouraging. Oh, I can't wait to begin! And then I shall have the extra pleasure of tutoring Harry," he added with a triumphant smirk.

Harry looked as if he could have done without that treat. Nobody spoke for a minute. Margaret gave the fire a poke; she was building a house in the embers for herself and Rupert, and they needed another window.

"Are you going to excavate the hill?" asked Rupert, who had plans of his own for putting Cormundy back on the map.

"Dear me, no! No, no, I shall just potter about, looking and listening."

"You've come in the nick of time," said the young man, stretching, and smiling in Margaret's direction.

"What do you mean?" asked Mr. Bogle with a sharp look.

"The village is dead all right, with people out of work, and buildings standing useless and empty. But one rich man could start the ball rolling again. Cormundy's a gift to a speculator; it won't be a backwater much longer!"

"You told me in your letter that you were a farmer." Mr. Bogle sounded quite put out.

"Yes, that's still true. We have meetings about the future of the village; people will discuss anything if we give them tea and buns. And they'll see reason in the end, I'm sure. But they've got so used to grousing, it's difficult for them to look ahead."

"There's a certain resistance to progress, is there?" asked Mr. Bogle with an involuntary grin.

"Well, I've only lived here two years, so they think I've a lot to learn. They'll be keen enough when they see how things work out. And everyone's delighted about *Mrs.* Musgrave," Rupert added, reaching for Margaret's hand, giving her a quick, warm smile. It was true that the Longshaws were popular in the village. So although Rupert had asked Margaret to marry him because he loved her, his engagement had raised his status by several notches.

Mr. Bogle beamed on him again, and exclaimed in a sort of ecstasy, "What it is to be young! I love the young with an *h*, because they're hopeful; with an *i*, because they're idealistic; with a *j*, because they're joyful; with a *k*, because they're kind! I love everything old, excepting people. There, I am inconsistent—I must confess to a weakness for the young. And now, to bed! Thank you for making me so much at home. It isn't often this old gentleman finds himself in such charming company!"

He pulled himself to his feet; his more agile shadow darted up the wall and across the ceiling. Margaret got up to escort him. "Good night, good night!" he cried, giving a fluttery movement of the hand. "The whole family, past and present, *and* the call to the avenger, all in the one room—quite a nucleus!" He followed Margaret out, closing the door softly behind him.

"He's bats, of course," said Harry, who tended to have a low opinion of his teachers.

"You mustn't call people bats just because they don't think the way you do," said Rupert in the older-brother voice he used when he took it upon himself to guide Harry. "Heyerdahl or Chay Blyth or any of your heroes must have seemed round the bend to begin with. Anyway, he's got every qualification under the sun, and he ought to be able to teach you a lot."

"I don't happen to believe in witches."

"What difference does that make? You'd better make the most of his stay, or you'll be hopelessly behind when you go back to school. Aren't you supposed to take "0" levels next year?"

"Don't preach," said Harry, tight-lipped.

"I'm not. But if you tell yourself he's bats you'll waste a lot of time, that's all, when your whole future depends on the next couple of years."

"Okay, okay. You've made your point."

Conscious of having done his duty, Rupert changed the subject. "I meant to tell you, I've put in an offer for the old mill."

Harry's eyes widened. "Whatever for?"

"I'm going to modernize it."

"That'll cost you a packet!"

"I'll make it pay." Rupert was leaning on the mantelpiece, resting his forehead against his hand. His face glowed in the firelight, as though his hopes and dreams showed through. His confidence roused a devil in Harry.

"You really think you're bringing peace and gladness to the natives, don't you?"

"They could do with it," said Rupert mildly. "You of all people know how demoralizing it is not to be able to fend for yourself. Well, I must go. It takes a good half hour to ride home."

"I didn't know you rode over."

Rupert remembered that Harry had loved to ride. He straightened and went to the door, pausing for a moment with one hand on the back of a chair. "Good night."

"Good night." Harry surveyed his attitude with a twisted smile, and added, "I can just see you in bronze, gratefully remembered in Cormundy Square."

"Shut up, you clot." And he left the room, reflecting, not for the first time, that illness had sharpened the wit of Harry.

He went downstairs. Margaret said, meeting him in the hall, "Mr. Bogle seems to love being here, which is so lucky. I'm sure he'll fit in. He didn't even want a bath."

"Harry's in a mood," said Rupert. "It's time he had a new companion."

"Tomorrow we could go into town and get some of our shopping done," she said, smoothing the lapels of his jacket. "We could have tea together."

He kissed the top of her head. "I'll call for you straight after lunch."

He opened the front door, and his black mare came forward to his whistle. He put his arms around Margaret. His horse patiently watched the embrace, but Mr. Bogle delicately closed his eyes. He had been listening to the conversation, clamped to the upstairs banister like a great bat.

Margaret stood in the doorway. It was too dark to see Rupert riding between the trees, but she knew by the sound of his horse's hooves when he reached the road. She waited until it died away in the distance.

Alone in his room, Harry maneuvered himself off the sofa and limped stiffly from chair to chair. His first action was to make sure the door was properly shut; he was ashamed of his unreliable legs. Resting a while on the arm of the chair where Mr. Bogle had been sitting, he drank the milk remaining with the tea things and stared into the grate. He decided that of all the people he knew, the one he most disliked was himself; and following that thought, he had to admit that the one he really admired was Rupert—he longed to be Rupert with all his soul. So he was obviously jealous of him, and that was a miserable thing to have on his conscience.

He heard Margaret coming down the passage. He could bind her to himself by complaining about the pain in his legs; if she belonged to Rupert, it was because he allowed it. She entered the room.

"Are you going to bed now?" she asked.

"In a minute."

She looked at him searchingly, but her face was bright with love. He was stabbed with self-pity.

"I suppose Rupert told you I was rude to him," he said.

"No, he didn't mention it. Don't worry. He can take it." She picked up the tea tray. "Did you finish the milk?"

"Yes. Why? Does it matter?"

"It was all there was until morning. Never mind." She sidled out with the tray. "Sleep well. Don't let Mr. Bogle's wild ideas give you nightmares."

"They won't. Good night."

All the same, the writing across the mantelpiece had

taken on a new significance. He felt very tired, and cold; he hunched closer to the fire, brooding over the evening.

Then he noticed a piece of paper lying under the skirt of Mr. Bogle's chair. It appeared to be blank, and he was about to throw it into the grate when his eye was caught by a translucent pattern on it against the firelight, something like the watermark on writing paper. It was a face, with antlers; at first glance he took it for a stag's head. But the eyes were not those of an animal. The longer he looked at it, the more it seemed that somebody was staring up at him through the paper.

He had to make an effort to put it on the fire. As it flared and vanished, it occurred to him that it must have belonged to Mr. Bogle; but even so he was glad to have got rid of it. The room seemed to relax, and now he heard Margaret moving about next door, singing softly as she got ready for bed.

Rupert had given Harry a stick, but he never used it. He could tell from a glance at the placing of the furniture whether he could cross a room on his worst days. He fetched his pajamas without much difficulty and undressed on the hearth. He turned off the lamp; at once the flame light took over, caressing the old room, bringing it more intimately to life. The ancestors, gently reflecting the movement of the fire, seemed to converge on its glow. Harry looked for a log but the basket was empty. Another thing illness had taught him was the burning time of wood; he reckoned his room would be dark within an hour.

He felt vulnerable, alone at night. He had been told that his legs would get better; but it would have taken a miracle to convince him of this in the dark, when any progress made during the day seemed to slip away and he was haunted by images of his hobbling self, or worse, crutches and a wheelchair. These were real torments that he would have been ashamed to share, even with easygoing Margaret, who was the first to suggest he needed a rest, or a meal in bed.

That evening as he sat on the hearthrug, he kept his imagination to heel by traveling round the house. To begin with, he had to pick out the ticking of the water cistern at the far end of the passage, like a tiny heart in the dark; then the dividing walls dwindled until he could make himself aware of every detail in the sleeping rooms. From the stairhead he saw that the moon was already high enough to stare through the little glass dome at its own marbled face on the hall floor. Glancing into the kitchen, he roused the cat enough to make it purr; but mice were scampering behind the books in the library. Going outside in his mind, he felt the rough stone mounting block under his hand. He could hear the grass crimp in the frost, and the fall of a stiff leaf. An owl called from the wood; with hardly a spring he could look into its nest, and the nests where rooks dozed like shabby clerks. The inhabited treetops smelt of vermin.

He was almost asleep when he went to bed, and his room was quite dark and chilly. The last thing that came into his mind was the writing under the mantelpiece. Mr. Bogle was speaking it aloud in Latin. *Exoriare aliquis nostris ex ossibus ultor;* his voice echoed through the house and shook the gloomy tapestries of night.

At that moment, in fact, Mr. Bogle was peacefully engaged in making up his diary. He sat at the desk, his glasses pushed up his forehead and glinting in the lamplight like an extra pair of watchful eyes. Occasionally he paused in his work to smile and rub his big hands together, as if he could not quite contain some secret satisfaction.

Mr. Bogle's diary was as large as an account book, with his initials in gilt on the cover: W.B. Looking forward to its discovery and publication, he indulged in many quotations, arguments and elaborate descriptions. He dabbled in all the arts, but the subtlety of words appealed to him most. "The pen is mightier than the sword," he had inscribed in flowery capitals on the title page. It was not his own thought: indeed he was never original; but he made up for that by using very complicated language.

He wound up his night's work with the word "Harry," underlined and followed by a number of question marks. He reread the page, smiling; then turned to the back of the book where he hoarded his press cuttings. On the top was a copy of an advertisement. It had been inserted in *The Times*, and ran:

> SCHOLARLY GENTLEMAN of modest tastes, engaged in research work, requires short-term board and lodging in exchange for light tutorial duties.

From a number of replies he had selected Rupert's, and on the whole he was pleased with his choice.

He allowed himself a glance through the other cuttings, some of them even illustrated; then, with a self-denying sigh, he closed the book and got up from the desk. He went to the window. The curtains were open, and he did not draw them now, but raised his arms to rest his hands on opposite sides of the frame. His coat did not fit properly; seen from behind, the breadth of his shoulders tapering into outstretched sleeves had the look of sable wings.

The wood pressed against this side of the house. The nearest trees actually rubbed the window, squeaking in any draft like chalk on a blackboard. Mr. Bogle did not mind them. Absorbed in his own reflection, he was making nightmare faces at himself in the glass. He seemed joined to the darkness of the wood through the openings of his mouth and eyes.

At last he stopped his game and turned back into the room, baby-bland again and smiling. He crossed to his bed and lay down, still in his clothes. On his bedside table he had arranged a cheap alarm clock, an ordnance survey map of the district, and a framed copy of his family tree. This was an intricate affair, written very small in black ink decorated with tongues of flame. Two or three coronets embellished its most illustrious branches. He studied it affectionately, repeating some favorite names to himself; and sniffed at the vase of flowers—he adored chrysanthemums—before folding his spectacles and turning off the light. Presently he too slept, laid out like that on the bedspread, slightly snoring with his mouth open, his breath puffs visible in the freezing air.

2

At Fury Wood the day began with the arrival of the postman. There was no slit for mail in the front door; he threw the letters down on the step, tugged at the bell, and bicycled away. From long experience he was able to do this poised with one foot on the pedal. The bell jangled through the old body of the house, like a toothache, at half past eight. Margaret brought Harry his breakfast on a tray at nine, and lessons did not start until ten, so there was no need for him to hurry. By the time he limped downstairs, Mr. Bogle had already organized the morning's work. He was a conscientious teacher; indeed, any contract entered into with him was always scrupulously kept on his part.

Harry had a quick brain and a good memory. He was used to praise at school, so he was disconcerted to find himself no match for Mr. Bogle's syllabus. He would set to work with confidence on a problem that looked familiar; but sooner or later even this old friend sprouted so many complications that he had to give up in despair. Luckily, Mr. Bogle enjoyed explaining things, and attacked each point with such enthusiasm that Harry suspected he had written the textbooks himself. He never stooped to a mere solution, but indulged in academic flights that left his unfortunate pupil far behind, feeling stupider than ever.

Mr. Bogle always wore a sheet of blotting paper tucked under his chin like an enormous bib, as a protection against his own writing which, like his eating, covered the adjacent surfaces with spots and blots. Letters came for him every morning, and he had a way of spreading his correspondence in front of people with fewer friends; he took up two-thirds of the table. He used an old quill pen, and an inkstand made out of a goat's hoof with a fringe of coarse black hair. The kitchen cat had taken a fancy to him; it was usually purring on his knees or under his chair.

Then there was Mrs. Gallops. She would have distracted even the most dedicated scholar. She came in every day to cook, and was a stout widow of a vengeful nature, with a greasy, yellowish complexion like old pudding. She made a continual clatter in the kitchen next door, as if her recipes had metallic ingredients, and swiped and banged about the stove, which she filled regularly with avalanches of coal. An hour before lunch, they knew from the smells what it was going to be, and what kind of individual twist it was getting from Mrs. Gallops. Even the food shrank from her tempers. The fish clung to its bones, the potatoes and custard to the bottoms of the pans. Harry had had enough of lunch before it came to the table.

Mr. Bogle was an arrant snob, with an insatiable appetite for stories about the Longshaws' grander friends. Harry discovered this on the very first morning, when he found himself being pumped about Rupert; so he invented a fantastic circle of acquaintances, partly to while away the time, partly to see just how much the tutor would swallow. It seemed he could take anything, even the octogenarian duchess with her epileptic butler, and her bath chair drawn by a pack of hounds; or Tibby Hopkins the albino millionaire, with his amazing collection of eggs. It was surprisingly easy to elaborate on the lives of these fabulous characters; and when Harry had made a mess of an exercise it soothed his soul to see how Mr. Bogle hung on his words, avid for every detail.

He had a headache one day, when Mr. Bogle had been with them for about a week, and he went upstairs right after lunch. It was a fine afternoon, and he sat looking out of the window across the fields which flowed for miles if the day was clear, though rain pushed the horizon nearer. The far groves planted as windbreaks looked stark and beautiful with most of their leaves gone, while close to the house in Fury Wood, the autumn color clung like a sprinkling of rust to the grim frames of the elms. A rook flapped across, gripping in its beak a bit of bread as big as a letter; Mrs. Gallops was profligate with scraps. Harry had let his mice out to exercise inside his jersey, and they were exploring him with their usual interest, when he heard steps he recognized as Rupert's coming down the passage toward his room.

"Hallo, what's up?"

"I had a headache."

"Bad luck," said Rupert, sitting down on the end of the bed. "How is it now?"

"Gone."

"Slacking off, were you?"

"No, as a matter of fact."

The pigeon flew up from the wood, gliding the last of the distance to alight faultlessly on the sill. Harry opened the window and it hobbled inside. A sneaky east wind flickered about the room.

"Has Mr. Bogle found any witches yet?" asked Rupert, after a silence.

"I haven't a clue. Where's Margaret?"

"At the farm, measuring for curtains. She's been biting my head off. How about a trip to the village? I could drop you there if you've anyone you want to visit." He paused; Harry did not answer. "Wasn't there a boy you used to like, one of the Shrewberrys? Why not look him up?"

"I can't just appear. He'll be busy."

"Give him a ring."

"They don't have a phone."

"Oh, come on, Harry, pull yourself together! You'll be a chronic invalid at this rate," said Rupert impatiently. And with a closer look, "For heaven's sake, take those creatures out of your sweater! I don't know how you can bear to have them running over you like that."

"It's my shirt they're running on."

"Then you'd better have a clean one." Rupert rummaged in the chest of drawers, threw a shirt across, and watched with a mixture of pity and exasperation as Harry changed his clothes. He frowned. "You ought to eat more."

"I can't, when Mrs. Gallops cooks it."

"Then she ought to be sacked!"

"We've tried. She won't go. Why don't you wait for me downstairs?" said Harry, angrily fumbling with buttons. "I'll join you in a minute."

"That's all right. I'll give you a hand down."

"I don't need your help!" Harry exclaimed, so passionately that Rupert was taken aback. He shrugged and left the room.

He had a sports car, a glamorous scarlet affair with the top down. A few minutes later Harry clambered in, grinning with pleasure. "Too cold for you?" Rupert shouted as the engine revved. He shook his head. The tree trunks whipped past. They slowed at the drive end, and turned up the road across open country.

The freshly plowed acres stretched away in ruled, converging furrows. Any remaining grass had been broken by frost to a watery green, as if a layer of glass divided it from the earth; and the cloudless sky had the same brittle texture. Cormundy Hill stuck up like the boss of a shield. The air was so clear, Harry could pick out the pinpoints of birds circling the tower. He was sitting with his eyes screwed against the wind and the speed, his lips in a fixed grin. But presently they were climbing in a lower gear between the terraces, to the square by the church where the summer visitors parked.

"I'll call for you in an hour or so," said Rupert, pulling up to Mrs. Shrewberry's door.

"Thanks." Harry got out, and rang the bell.

Old Mrs. Shrewberry had been squeezed dry by the cares of her numerous family. Her youngest son Tobias was Harry's age, while Matthew, her eldest, kept the Nag's Head. She had children and grandchildren dotted about the world, and now she peered at Harry framed in the doorway, as though he might be one of them arrived unexpectedly on a visit. Then she recognized him.

"Harry Longshaw, isn't it? Bless me, you've grown!

Turn into the light, let me look at you. This is a nice surprise; I heard you were still poorly. Did you walk up?"

"Rupert brought me." Harry was embarrassed by this scene on the step. A few doors along, outside Welsh's electrical shop, some men were dawdling to watch a football match on the television in the window. Mrs. Shrewberry's remarks had attracted their attention.

"Toby's not home from school yet," she said. "Can you call back later?"

"Okay. I'll do that." Harry turned and limped across the pavement. He wished she would shut the door; he could feel her gaze as if it were red-hot, and a battery of stares from the loitering men. He would have to wait in the church, and there was the square to cross.

"You can have a cup of tea, if you've nothing better to do," she called after him.

He hesitated, then went back. In the silence he noticed the crying of birds around the tower, as though the church had a voice.

"In here," said Mrs. Shrewberry, leading the way into the kitchen. "Sit down." She made a fuss of putting the kettle on, not looking at Harry, sucking in her lips with pity. "Rupert brought you, did he? Margaret's young gentleman?"

"That's right."

"When are they going to be married? Christmas Eve, is it?"

"Yes."

"And you're going to move in with them, on the Musgrave farm?"

"That's right."

"So you'll be selling the old place, I shouldn't wonder."

"We're trying to. It's difficult; the house is falling to bits, and there's just the wood, no other land."

Mrs. Shrewberry nodded. The undesirability of Fury Wood had been discussed in the village from the time of Margaret's engagement.

She reached for the tea caddy, which had a portrait of the Queen and Prince Philip on it, framed in broken parchment with an unfortunate resemblance to a paper hoop at the circus. The mugs, too, were stamped with royal heads. The kettle was the old-fashioned sort, balanced on the grate; the mantelpiece had a red-and-white-checked frill, and a display of postcards from the family abroad. Mrs. Shrewberry's mother had made the rag rugs, which had thickened underfoot to the consistency of old suits. The shadow of the church tower fell across the room all day; a pair of Java sparrows moped in their cage, and even the cat took no notice of them as a rule.

"I heard you had a vistor staying, a professor, someone said," Mrs. Shrewberry remarked as she handed Harry his tea.

"Yes. He's meant to tutor me. He's leaving at Christmas."

Mrs. Shrewberry considered this, while her busy eyes marked one or two people drifting across the square.

"I'm glad you're able to go on with your learning; Tobias always said you were clever. Now I wonder what's going on out there?" she said, craning over the sink to get a better view. "It's filling up like a summer day!" She stood on tiptoe, first on one foot, then on the other, steadying herself by the taps. "Well, I never, Harry!" she suddenly exclaimed. "Talk of the devil, isn't that your professor? Good gracious!"

A blackness flapped past the window, like an outsize rook in the wind. Harry moved up beside Mrs. Shrewberry; the cat leapt onto the sill among the mops and detergents. All three of them stared. After a while Mrs. Shrewberry said in a whisper, as though she might be heard out-of-doors, "He's doing the Horn Dance. I haven't seen that danced here for years."

Mr. Bogle did appear to be demonstrating, or practicing, some kind of dance. With odd, skipping steps he followed a winding, diagonal line, neatly avoiding with a loop the stumpy obelisk of the war memorial; he set to the right, set to the left, turned, and danced back. He had an audience of a dozen or so, all men, all known to Harry; they were grouped around the square, lounging against houses or the churchyard wall. Nobody talked, nobody smiled, though Harry thought the tutor cut an absurd figure with his spidery legs and flapping coat, curving up the square with his dance, prancing away with his pockets stuffed as usual with letters, his spectacles bobbing about on his nose, and his hands lifted up, palm to palm, as though he was carrying something. He felt a little embarrassed because Mr. Bogle was, in a sense, the responsibility of Fury Wood, and he looked at Mrs. Shrewberry, thinking to make a joke of it. To his surprise she was still watching the scene attentively. And the tramp who sat most of the day in the church porch sensed a happening and shambled near, picking his way between the graves.

"What do you mean, Horn Dance?" asked Harry, to break the spell.

"That's what it's called. Some say it dates back to Robin Hood and Maid Marian, and the men in Lincoln green. The last time I saw it was on Victory Day—over twenty-five years ago. Long before you were born. They started up at the church, and kept it going all night. And the bonfires! There was one in every field, as far as the eye could see; I can smell them now. And the bells! I thought the tower would fall. To tell you the truth there was a spot of trouble after; what with the victory, and the fires, and the beer flowing like water, things got out of hand. Mat was in the hospital a week; he had quite a nasty turn. He'd just moved into the Nag's Head, I remember."

"I suppose everybody got tight," said Harry.

"He wasn't behind the bar. Oh no, it was free for

all that night! Our Mat was one of the dancers."

Harry glanced back to the square. Mr. Bogle was still performing solo. The watching men were not drawn in, though none of them moved away. The butcher and his son had come out of their shop. They had scraped pink skins and blue eyes; Titmuss Junior had a knife sticking out of his apron, like a dagger. Poor Peter Quotter joined them. He was watching Mr. Bogle's antics with astonishment.

"Rupert's hiring Quotter as a stockman," said Harry. "Did you know he was fetching in bullocks next month?"

But Mrs. Shrewberry was still riveted to the square. "How he does go at it at his age! You'd never think such a tall gent would have so much kick in him. Funny how it draws the men. Now who's this pushing up, blocking the view?" She tapped sharply on the pane. A moment later she exclaimed, in quite a different tone, "Tobias! What are you doing, hanging about there? Come in at once for your tea!"

The front door slammed, and Tobias entered the kitchen, looking sheepish. He nodded at Harry, tossed his school cap onto the dresser, and thrust his hands, then his face under the taps. He had a dish of macaroni and cheese for his tea; Harry, an unexpected guest, had to make do with bread and butter. At last his stomach growled so loudly that Tobias noticed it.

"Do you want a bit?"

"Can't you eat it all?"

"I've had enough; go ahead."

Harry took the bowl and spoon, and ate like a wolf until it was finished. Tobias watched him, surprised. And a year's reserve suddenly vanished.

When tea was over they went out by the back door and sat down on the step. It was sheltered there, though they could see for miles. The horizon palely echoed the invisible sea. Tobias took out a cigarette and bent his face to the match.

"Remember the cart?"

"Sure," said Harry.

Tobias squatted, smoking, apparently deep in thought. At last he ground out the stub, got up and sloped to the shed, and pulled out the cart with an abstracted air. It was only a plank on wheels. Tobias worshipped speed; next year he would be able to have a motorbike. "I'll run you home," he suggested. The Fury road was the steepest out of the village.

They had to avoid Mrs. Shrewberry, but Tobias excelled at that. They pulled the cart round behind the houses, and at the top of the hill they sat down back to back. Tobias was behind with his knees against his chest, though he could drag his feet for a brake. Harry was steering, with a precipitous view of the fall of the road below them; after the sober planes of home, his breath tightened with excitement.

Tobias gave a shove, and they were off. The cart quickly gathered speed. They tore past the council houses, the pumps, the empty mill where Rupert's car was parked. They took the bend on a couple of wheels; and there was an obstacle rushing upon them, a van waiting on their side of the road. Harry passed it by the skin of his teeth, missing by inches a truck that was steaming up the hill; and then with his heart still in his mouth he could see that the road was clear, and they sailed down whooping with triumph. The cart was carried by its own momentum some yards along the flat before it slackened and stopped. The van trundled past; the driver sitting so primly in his cab crowned the glory of the ride.

They went on to Fury Wood, at a walking pace with Tobias doing all the pushing because Harry's legs had seized up. By and by, they turned into the drive between the tree trunks which towered overhead, fanning at last very high up like clusters of Gothic columns. Tobias could see that Harry was getting cold, and he tried to hurry, but the spongy ground made it difficult to push. Harry crouched on the cart, locked in his own discomfort. Tobias sat down suddenly behind him, out of breath.

"That was my tutor, dancing in the square," Harry said then.

"I know, he's a friend of Mat's. You're driving him to drink, I expect. What's his name again?"

"Bogle."

"It suits him."

They came out of the wood in front of the house. The evening had grown appreciably darker; the rooks were making their usual racket before going to bed. "Dirty things, those birds," said Tobias, wiping his face with his hand.

"They bring you luck."

Tobias could have argued with that, he knew the Longshaw history; but he did not speak again until they were passing the pump. Then he asked, "What's that for?"

"You can see what it's for." Harry's teeth were chattering; he ached to be indoors.

"I can see the pump. What's that stone for behind it?"

"It's a mounting block."

"It's not," said Tobias with conviction. "A mounting block that height would have at least one step to it."

"All right, then it's to stand a bucket on, or scrub washing on. I don't know what it's for. Do get a move on; or shall I crawl the rest of the way?"

"It's got blood on it," pronounced Tobias.

"Rust, you mean." But Harry looked at the block, to make sure. There was a reddish stain on it, sunk deep into the stone. "Copper," he said. The only odd thing about it was that he had never noticed it before.

"Door-to-door service," said Tobias, stopping at the front step.

Harry hauled himself up. "You needn't take the cart back," he said when he had got his breath. "Shove it in the stable."

"Righto. You know it's Guy Fawkes Day on Saturday; will you be coming up to the village?"

"Rupert and Margaret won't; he's fixed a meeting for the Fifth."

Tobias shook his head. "Why's he picked bonfire night? Last year the whole village turned out in the square. He'd better change the date of his meeting."

"I'll tell him. So long. Thanks for the ride."

Tobias ran round the corner of the house, doubled up with the cart whizzing in front of him.

The hall felt like a tomb. A theatrical wallpaper had been used in all the best rooms, and this one had brown marble pillars, potted plants and cages of birds. At twilight these fantasies appeared real, but there was nothing to help Harry to the stairs. He staggered round the edge, upsetting the umbrella stand with a crash.

Mr. Bogle was out for supper. Considering the trouble he took to be pleasant, his absence was strangely welcome. Margaret cooked sausages on the fire in Harry's room, and they ate them straight from the pan, as soon as they were cool enough, in their fingers.

"Did you see the Bogle dancing in the square?" Harry asked as they finished.

"*Mr. Bogle*, dancing?" exclaimed Rupert and Margaret together.

"Yes, he was at it all afternoon, hopping about like an old goat."

At that moment, they heard the front door slam.

And at once Harry felt uncomfortable, as though Mr. Bogle could have been eavesdropping. Nobody spoke. Mr. Bogle came upstairs and paused on the landing. Then he went into his room and shut the the door. They heard all this quite clearly. He might even have been making his steps louder for their benefit.

"What do you mean, *dancing*?" said Margaret in a low voice. "I'm sure he's never done such a thing in his life!"

"Don't you believe it!" said Harry. "That pompous manner is all a sham. He was really sent; it was something called a Horn Dance." And then out of the blue he remembered the bit of paper he had found, with the pattern on it. He stopped short, frowning.

"I've seen that danced," said Rupert. "The people in front carry antlers. It's quite impressive."

"Was anyone dancing with Mr. Bogle?" asked Margaret.

"No," said Harry. "But Mrs. Shrewberry couldn't take her eyes off him; she'd have been out there herself for two pins."

"She couldn't have danced with him. Women aren't allowed to join in any of the Morris dances," said Rupert.

"Oh, indeed! Why ever not? I should like to see you stop me, if I wanted to!" said Margaret with spirit.

Mr. Bogle sat in his room in the dark. He heard Rupert leave the house, and he waited a little longer to give Margaret and Harry time to go to bed. Then he glided into the passage. He wore a full gown of tabby cat skins over his everyday clothes; like a dusky ghost he sped downstairs and crossed the shadowy hall without a sound. He went into the library and closed the door softly behind him.

The bookcases were heavy with Victorian literature, complete editions of Scott, Dickens, Macaulay, with a smell of crumbly hide. Mr. Bogle snuffed it up, grinning; and then he struck a match and lit the candle he had placed in readiness on the table. His face hung within the globe of light as he paused again to savor the secrecy of the scene.

He stepped to the window and, drawing back the curtain, raised the sash. Three figures were waiting outside, jumpy in the cold. He laid a finger on his lips as they climbed into the room, and as he rearranged the curtain, eyed them over his shoulder.

In these surroundings anyone would have looked furtive, and Mr. Bogle's friends were no exception. They lurked self-consciously in the shadows, starting when a late arrival tapped on the pane. But now they were all present, and Mr. Bogle produced one of his suitcases from a corner and lifted it onto the table. The click of the lock sounded like a pistol shot in the close room. Everyone moved forward; the little pool of candlelight was hemmed in by expectant faces.

Mr. Bogle's suitcase contained a number of carefully-packed, brightly colored clothes. His hands moved deftly among them with a tailor's instinct, as he shook them out for the approval of his friends.

"Ladies first," he said, holding up a striped skirt, a cloak with jet trimming, and a black lace cap. "People trace our heroine back to Maid Marian, but she has other, more ancient titles. We'll call her the Betty," and he turned to Rackstraw, the man on his right, who had lately wound up his wasted farm by selling his land to Rupert, and on whose face the scowls of a lifetime were grimly etched.

"You won't catch *me* dressed as a woman!" he retorted, glaring round at his mates in case any of them dared to joke about it.

Far away, in Harry's deep unconsciousness, the word "rats" registered.

"Hush, we mustn't rouse the house," said Mr. Bogle. "To interrupt their innocent slumbers would be unforgivable; it's a pity we can't meet earlier than this. You will be the Bet, I say, and as for passing yourself off as a woman, that doesn't enter into it; in fact I want you to let your beard grow."

Rackstraw looked at the skirt with distaste. "There's a button off."

"You won't, of course, do anything rash, such as asking your wife or daughter to sew it on," Mr. Bogle told him smoothly. "Preserve the decencies with safety pins. And find an old parasol to complete your costume. Now for you, Mat. I see you as the hobby horse."

Mat Shrewberry was a blue-eyed, fair-skinned man,

bald to the ears. If life turned kinder he might age into a jolly Friar Tuck figure; he had been a great one for practical jokes in his youth. He was still blushing because it was his fault that the meetings had to be so late; he was busy at the Nag's Head until eleven, and then he had to wait until his wife slept. He had been henpecked from birth. There was an excitable streak in his nature which the women in his life distrusted.

Mat's costume had a skirt built out on a frame to make the head and body of a caparisoned horse. False legs in red silk stockings hung down on either side. Mat's own legs would make the horse run and prance; his body would appear to belong to the red legs. The horse frame was bent from being packed, and its paper head needed painting.

"Get into it, my dear fellow!" Mr. Bogle encouraged him. "Try it on!" And everyone watched with a serious face while Mat struggled into his costume and adjusted its leather braces. "A perfect fit; it might have been made for you. Titmuss and Welsh, these are yours." Mr. Bogle passed them tunics and stockings of Lincoln green. Welsh nodded and grinned. He was the man Mr. Bogle had spoken to when he had arrived in Cormundy. Titmuss the butcher held his tunic against himself in dismay. He was a giant of a man; it was several sizes too small.

"I could put in a gusset," he said doubtfully. He worked tapestry in his spare time, gentle garden scenes. He thought he could manage gussets.

"Certainly not!" said Mr. Bogle. "This is a serious happening, you know, not a rustic carnival." He dived again into the suitcase, and produced a dark robe with wide sleeves.

"That doesn't appeal to me," said Titmuss. "It's drab, isn't it?"

"Nonsense, man," said Mr. Bogle, who could not bear his friends to disagree with him. "My own dress will be somber. In this you will have a significant part to play; you will become my instrument, the Instrument of the Avenger. Besides, I shall obtain an ornament for you later on, before the night. Now," he said, shutting the case, and resting his hands palms downward on the lid, "you're sure you can keep these things hidden from your wives? The dears have their drawbacks, when there is a happening afoot."

There was a general murmur of agreement, even from the blushing Mat.

"We'll have our rehearsals, of course," said Mr. Bogle, "but they won't be dress rehearsals. Bring the ladies; they're welcome to come along. I daresay you'll find they aren't much interested. And that's it, for the time being. But I'll keep in touch."

He pulled back the curtain and opened the window. The men clambered up one by one, and dropped down into the dark garden; huge Titmuss cursed as he struggled in the frame. Mr. Bogle frowned and drew the curtain behind him. He disliked the habit of swearing. People were too apt to take his own name in vain.

3

The trophy room got its name from the animal heads on the walls, mute witnesses to the aim of sporting Longshaws. It was a later addition to Fury Wood, separated from the main block by a dusty conservatory. Margaret and Harry never used it, though it contained some stiff furniture upholstered in tattered silk; in that room more than anywhere else they felt aware of the decaying house. Outside, the laurels crammed against the walls, pressing the backs of their leaves against the windows.

But the trophy room appealed to Mr. Bogle. It seemed to him the right place for a dance; and with Margaret's permission that was where he practiced his steps, as solemnly as though the branched chandeliers still hung in all their glory under the ceiling. Sometimes

Margaret and Rupert caught sight of him through the window when they returned home late. From his courtly behavior he might have been surrounded by a crowd of friends. They never laughed at his dancing again; kind Margaret in particular was deeply touched by his solitude.

Harry remembered to warn Rupert to change the date of his meeting; but he was skeptical.

"Guy Fawkes is for kids, Harry. It won't make any difference to us."

"Toby said the square was full last year."

"Oh, I daresay; but last year there was nothing else on."

Harry said no more. He thought Rupert misjudged the spirit of the village. It was more willing, and more obstinate than he realized.

The meeting was to take place at Rupert's farm beyond Cormundy. Margaret spent all morning baking refreshments; Harry liked hearing her in the kitchen. The year was drawing to an end, and even the finest weather had lost some of its brilliance; the light was on in the room where he sat grappling with geometry. Mr. Bogle was opposite, as usual. He seemed to gain in substance from the ebbing days; he quite bulged behind the table. And his belongings obtruded more, especially the goat's-hoof inkstand. Harry could not help looking at it; and once or twice, when he thought he was concentrating particularly hard on a problem, he found himself actually drawing it in his exercise book.

Mr. Bogle was writing to a titled friend. He had a habit of mouthing his thoughts. "Your Grace" was several times repeated.

"You aren't writing to the Dumbbell of Clock, by any chance?" Harry asked, losing patience.

Mr. Bogle paused, and looked expectantly across at him.

"He's an uncle of mine, by marriage," said Harry carelessly. "He used to own half of Scotland, whole mountains and lochs, you know how they do up there."

"Friends of mine near Edinburgh—" began Mr. Bogle.

"Further north than Edinburgh," interrupted Harry relentlessly. "Anyhow, you couldn't have found a quieter man, until August the Twelfth one year. They were out on the moors when the Dumbbell suddenly went out of his mind, took up his gun and shot them all dead—gillies, beaters, the houseparty he'd invited for the occasion; there they all lay, dead as ducks in the heather. His poor wife," Harry continued, seeing Mr. Bogle about to speak, "known in her heyday as Clock's Dumb Belle, was luckily at home, or he would have done her in too. Odd, wasn't it? You'd never have picked him out in a crowd. The whole estate had to be sold for compensation."

"What a tragedy!" exclaimed Mr. Bogle. He took

off his glasses and wiped them on the end of his tie. He looked cleverer without them.

"It was, and it should never have happened," said Harry, glancing at his watch and seeing that lunch was only ten minutes away. "They had a plate which had been in the family for years, with 'A Gift from Delft, Beware the Twelfth' written on it. That was clear enough, and they should have been more careful."

"Yes, indeed. Who can afford to ignore an ancestral warning?" And Mr. Bogle added in his sonorous voice, " 'Arise, thou avenger to come, out of my ashes.' "

Harry stared. The familiar words seemed to swell in the room, until they hung like an incantation between himself and Mr. Bogle.

A particularly loud crash next door, Mrs. Gallops hurling plates into the oven, broke the silence. He pushed his exercise books across the table with his most charming smile. "I haven't been able to do very much this morning. Your problems are a bit beyond me, I'm afraid." He stood up awkwardly—he was always stiff after lessons—and limped across the room. He knew Mr. Bogle was watching him, and he suddenly wondered if he was going to lose his temper. And as he reached the door Mr. Bogle spoke with a venom Harry had never in his life heard before. "It's a pity you mocked the Horn Dance. It might have done you good."

Harry froze, completely at a loss. After a minute he looked round at the tutor, who had replaced his spectacles and returned to his correspondence. "Ours were the frolics of twin intellects," his lips silently formed the words.

Then the front doorbell rang, a jangling shock, and Margaret put her head into the room.

"Answer that, Harry, will you? I'm up to my eyes. Lunch, will be late, I'm afraid, Mr. Bogle."

"Don't let that worry you, my dear," he said in his deferential way, rising from his chair a few inches with a movement that oddly resembled a curtsy, upside down.

Harry crossed the hall and opened the front door. Two boys were waiting there, come to collect junk for the village bonfire. They scraped their boots on the step and followed Harry to the gun room, which Margaret was using as a storeroom. The guns had all been sold, but pale stripes on the walls showed where they had stood. A pair of carp in glass cases looked like fakes. There was a bundle of rubbish in a corner; one of the boys easily lifted it. They were both younger than Harry. He remembered them at school, skirmishing two years below him; impossibly childish they had seemed then.

He opened the cupboard under the stairs, where there was a box of worn-out clothes. A man was hanging inside.

Next instant he saw that of course it was not a real man. It was only a bolster buttoned up in a jacket and trousers. It had a face crudely painted on cardboard, and its neck was pulled in with string which was tied to a hook in the cupboard, so that the head lolled forward in a horribly realistic way. He recognized the clothes. The trousers were old ones of his, and the jacket was Rupert's. The sleeves and legs hung emptily from the stuffed torso.

Practical joke or booby trap or whatever it was meant to be, it rattled Harry. After what seemed minutes, his heart gave a sickening jolt and began beating again.

Behind him the boys got a bit of a scare, but then they laughed, and one of them unhooked the dummy. "He's great!" he said admiringly. "Did you make him?"

Harry shook his head. He called Margaret; his voice sounded less steady than he would have liked. She came into the hall, pink-faced from the stove, and stared at the boy clasping the dummy, which was taller than he was, with the cuffs of the trousers trailing on the floor. "What on earth's that?"

"It was hanging in the cupboard," said Harry.

"How did it get there?"

"I've no idea," he said.

There was a baffled silence.

"Mrs. Gallops," Margaret decided. She called, "Mrs. Gallops!"

The cook joined them. She stared at the dummy and walked all round it. Then she announced that she had never set eyes on it before, and offered to put this in writing if they liked, and swear to it. She had a way of forestalling trouble by invoking the law.

Margaret said kindly, "Perhaps you'd like it for the children's Guy Fawkes. That coat of Rupert's isn't fit to be seen, and Harry's grown out of the trousers. I don't want the bolster. If you've a use for it, take it home; if not, these boys can have it."

Mrs. Gallops replied that Guy Fawkes was for those who indulged in it; she had the next meal to get.

So the boys took the dummy and bicycled away. Margaret and Harry watched them go. The doubled-up figure strapped to the carrier looked just as ugly from behind, looming over the cyclist, its limp sleeves dangling.

"Mr. Bogle might have made it," Harry suggested. He could hear as he spoke how ridiculous he sounded.

"Why?"

"Oh, I don't know. A whim. A bagatelle."

"It was Mrs. Gallops," said Margaret. "I'm certain of it. She's helped herself before."

There were no lessons on Saturday afternoons. Margaret had finished baking, and after lunch she carried her sewing machine into Harry's room and worked there; she was making her wedding dress. The chairs and bed were spread with the material: white cotton sprigged with green like a snowy garden. She tacked seams and darts with her mouth full of pins; sometimes she got up and held the dress against herself, viewing her reflection in the glass over the mantelpiece with a critical eye. The old-fashioned sewing machine hummed in the room like a hive of bees. Harry lay on his bed and read, sometimes raising his head to watch her. And the grouped ancestors also watched, the ladies with interest, the gentlemen with tolerant, disengaged expressions.

"Why don't you like Mr. Bogle?" asked Margaret out of the blue.

Harry fumbled for words. He had learnt to be wary of discussing the tutor in private; too often he was caught by evidence that Mr. Bogle had overheard.

"Why do you?" he returned evasively.

"Let's say that I don't *dis*like him, poor old boy. I think he's a bit pathetic. But you make it pretty obvious that you can't get on with him at all, so I wondered what you'd got against him."

"Nothing," said Harry.

"Let's face it, it's probably all tied up with Rupert and me," said Margaret, bending over the machine to thread it.

"How do you mean?"

"All this." She gestured over the draped cotton. "You're bound to feel a bit—well, I don't know. Left out, perhaps." She paused, expecting Harry to argue, but he said nothing. He was deeply hurt. She went on, "I just wanted to say, don't take it out on Mr. Bogle. After all, he does his best to please you; you can twist him round your little finger."

In the silence the machine whirred cozily.

"You know I'm pleased about Rupert."

"Of course." Margaret pulled the thread and clipped it. "But then there's the move on top of everything else. It's an awful upheaval for you. As a matter of fact it was Mr. Bogle who pointed all this out to me in the beginning. So maybe he understands you better than you think."

"He's no right to discuss me with you," said Harry furiously. "He hasn't a clue how I feel."

Margaret shook out the dress and stood up, and holding it against her shoulders, checked the hang of it with the preening movements of a bird. "How does it look?" she asked. She had a knack of changing the subject to stave off a row. Harry suspected her of doing the same in her mind; now he guessed that she might be covering up her own dislike of Mr. Bogle because it suited her to have him at Fury Wood. She could go out as often as she wanted with a clear conscience. He glanced at her as angrily as if he had already proved this; and at the same time he despised himself for spying out a motive she wanted to hide.

"I don't know how you can listen to that ass Bogle," he said. "He doesn't talk about *you* behind *your* back; he knows what I'd say if he did."

"It's miles too big," Margaret decided. "I shall have to take in all the darts. Do you think lace, or *broderie anglaise*? Lace would be cheaper. Two feet a sleeve and two for the collar; I wish you'd help—how much is that altogether?"

"Two yards," he said, against his will.

"Call it three, to be on the safe side." And Margaret made a note on a piece of paper. He could tell from her expression that as far as she was concerned, the conversation had gone according to plan. There was no point in trying to justify himself anymore; he went on with his book.

All the same the argument lingered like a bad taste in his mouth, spoiling the rest of the afternoon. At half past six he got into the car, while Margaret filled the back seat with cake tins and crockery. It was a good night for fireworks, clear and still. Harry stared coldly at the opposite trees. Margaret said, "You might hold this. It'll get dented otherwise, if I have to stop suddenly." He took the empty tea urn on his knees.

She did not speak again until they reached the village square. Then she stopped, and he got out. There were several people about, waiting for the fun to start; some boys were already lighting sparklers in a corner. Margaret put her head out of the window and asked whether anyone wanted a lift to the meeting at the Musgrave farm. Nobody did, so she waved to Harry and drove on alone.

The church and houses seemed to move closer in the dusk, as if they too were drawn to the bonfire in the middle of the square. It was as high as the first floor windows, and still growing; little boys kept running in with last-minute junk, clambering up and down like imps, stacking the heap. At last they crowned it with the dummy from Fury Wood, which they had tied to a broken-down chair. Harry saw them hoisting its dark shape against the sky, and he looked quickly away.

Mr. Bogle was standing by the churchyard wall, holding his violin loosely by the neck while he scratched his head with the bow. There were several men with him, talking together. Bogle was half a head taller than anyone else, but he did not show that he noticed Harry, who moved at once to put the bulk of the bonfire between them. All this time people were drifting up the slopes into the square. Mat Shrewberry pushed past, his eyes busy with the middle distance, his jacket open and smelling faintly of beer. Peter Quotter was hovering about a chest on which a supply of fireworks had been laid, mostly rockets and Roman candles. Every year he was allowed to set them off; he got as much pleasure from them as a child.

Tobias came up with a group of friends, and Harry began to enjoy himself. High overhead the stars were pricking, freckling the sky between the roofs, spanning the depth beyond the church with beasts and heroes.

Someone put a match to the fire. The first flame wavered, weak in the dark; then it broke free with a quick blue swallowing edge. It touched paraffin, shot orange and red, and fell back on the surrounding rubbish with fierce and flickering tongues.

Peter Quotter opened his display with rockets and Roman candles. They were all thinking the rockets were duds, when up they shot with a whistling gasp, and bursting high over the housetops, let down their pink and green streamers. The squat Roman candles blazed, and spat sparks. Quotter's face in the glare was loving and attentive, the face of a man at prayers.

By now the square was packed with people, and Harry suddenly wondered whether anyone at all had gone to Rupert's meeting. Everybody was concentrating on the fireworks, and Quotter, conscious of being just once a year the center of attention, was making the most of them. He ended the show with a crescendo of rockets; the faces all turned whitely up to watch them explode. People whistled and shouted at the leisurely falling stars. When the noise subsided, a hoarse dog continued to bark, chained up in somebody's cold garden.

All this time the fire was striking inward to the heart of the pyre. Some children were gingerly pushing potatoes to bake in the hot ash at the edge. Whenever a flame leapt, its grotesque reflection licked the heads of the crowd; but the dummy remained cool on his throne at the top.

Mr. Bogle tucked his fiddle under his chin and began to play. It sang like a human voice. Mat Shrewberry and some other men started dancing at one end of the square, with a lot of clapping and stamping, while a larger group joined hands in a ring round the bonfire. Harry moved back against the shelter of a wall. He caught glimpses of Tobias and his friends, whirling first this way, then that; and he watched the progress of the fire. He noticed that the bolster dummy had caught a spark and begun to smolder; and he suddenly wished, for no logical reason, that it was not wearing his and Rupert's clothes. They gave him a personal interest in its punishment.

Now everyone in the square was hotly illuminated. There was a constant traffic to and from the Nag's Head, and cheering to encourage the dancers. In any lull the flames took over with their fiery throats. The reek of gunpowder still hung in the air.

Harry's attention was divided between the dummy, and a man dancing alone near the fire. He noticed him particularly because he did not recognize him, and strangers were rare in Cormundy during the winter. Besides, he leapt and twisted with such extraordinary agility; and sensing Harry's admiration, he stayed just in front of him to show off the finer points of his performance. He was an odd-looking fellow: very dark, with curious tufted hair and a pronged beard. Whenever he leapt, his jacket flew up, and his belt was hung all round with rabbit skins which flapped too. He looked like the barbaric spirit of the scene.

But then Harry forgot him, because Rupert and Margaret were walking across the churchyard. He waved, and in a few moments they joined him.

"What on earth's going on?" said Margaret. "We could see the glow for miles. What is this—Walpurgis Night?"

"They're all as drunk as owls, as tight as ticks!"

Rupert sounded angry. "If I'd known this was how they kept the Fifth of November, I'd never have fixed the meeting."

"Nobody came," Margaret told Harry. "Not a single person. What's got into them all? This didn't happen last year; this is a riot. Someone has stood them a lot of beer. Just look at old Bogle, fiddling away for dear life! At least his party has some sort of order about it."

At that moment Mr. Bogle stopped playing. He bowed and smiled to the crowd, with the exalted expression of a café minstrel, and directed a gay wave of his bow at the party from Fury Wood. His dancers wiped their faces and loosened their ties, seeming a little self-conscious in front of their wives and friends. Then Mr. Bogle put up his fiddle again, and started a different tune. It was a lilting, up-and-down melody, ancient as the earth, leading away and away, winding like a goat track into a distant country. He established this strange air with his hollow instrument, and everyone in the square fell still; even the beer-drinking part of the crowd paused with the mugs halfway to their mouths. And near Harry someone said, under his breath, "That's a sweet tune."

Mr. Bogle's dancers lined up behind him, fitting their steps to the sound. The nearest spectators pressed back. Easily, lightly, the dance began, the old dance, the Horn Dance; and everyone watched, everyone listened. Now Harry remembered with astonishment that at first it had struck him as ridiculous. The concentration of the crowd was impressive. They might have been turned to stone under the fluid light and shadow of the fire.

But they were interrupted by a blazing burst, as the dummy went up in a sheet of flame. The spell broke: there was a roar from the people in the square and they surged forward. Next moment something collapsed unexpectedly in the heart of the fire, and the dummy began to topple and tumble down the red-hot ashes. Those at the back were still pushing to see, while the front ranks struggled to get clear with screams as if they were already burnt. In the nick of time, the menace broke into fiery pieces, a second before any damage was done. And Margaret realized that she was gripping Rupert's arm. They were all three as white as paper.

"Let's get out of here," said Rupert. "This way, Harry. We had to leave the car at the bottom, the crowd's so thick."

The shadow of the church drenched them. The whine of the Horn tune followed them to the car. But Mr. Bogle had lost his rapt audience; people were making a joke of the dummy, and beer was circulating freely.

Nobody spoke on the way back to Fury Wood. Rupert was depressed, and Margaret and Harry kept a sympathetic silence. As they turned into the drive, Harry glanced back. Cormundy looked like a monstrous firework smoldering in the darkness; he thought he could catch echoes of the crowd even at that distance.

When he got out of the car he was surprised by the height of trees, the far and frosty sky.

Very late that night, when the moon lay like a catch in the branches of an elm, a man stepped out of cover into the blue and silver strip before the house. He cast a long, spook-shaped shadow, tipped with his tufted hair like two little horns. He stared round, quite at his ease, with his legs apart and his thumbs tucked into his belt; then he walked lightly to the block and rested his right hand on it as he stood there looking down.

The shriek of an owl roused him. He crossed the clearing and disappeared into the wood.

4

The dawn wind rolled breakers against the coast, and clouds across the plain. As the sun mounted the invisible east, it began to pelt with rain; in Cormundy the roads turned into streams with a scum of ash and charred litter that stoppered the chuckling drains.

Peter Quotter had scorched himself, and he went to church that morning on two sticks, swinging one leg, with the foot in a gouty bandage. The congregation was smaller than usual, the vicar noted as he climbed to the pulpit to deliver his sermon. Month after month he was discouraged by the passive, disillusioned faces; he was careful to choose comfortable words, fixing his eyes meanwhile on the triumphant rose window.

Margaret played the organ; Harry and Rupert joined her in the singing, leading an uneven chorus from the back pews. This was in the family tradition. Victorian Longshaws had had the church restored, carved the eagle spreading its wings for the Bible, given vestments and stained glass. Tablets to their memory lined one wall of the chancel. Under them, in an alcove, a stone crusader lay at rest, his head on a bolster, his hands folded on his naked sword, his feet neatly propped against a faceless beast—a ferret perhaps. His castle had disappeared, but his bony, ascetic profile had survived the generations, even to his descendant Harry, who was keeping himself upright by gripping the front of the pew; his legs always felt worse when it rained, and the last hymn seemed to go on forever.

Amen was sung, and the vicar smiled into space as he returned to the vestry. Margaret shut the creaking instrument. Someone opened the great door, and an icy chill struck the length of the nave. The rain could be heard splashing on the paving outside the porch. Everyone had something to say about the weather, but as soon as Rupert appeared they escaped into it. Only Mrs. Shrewberry was left, struggling with her umbrella.

"Queer goings-on last night," Rupert remarked as he opened it up for her.

"They don't know when to stop, and that's the truth," she readily agreed. "Nobody minds fireworks, but that dancing was uncalled for. Frightening the old folk in their beds at one and two in the morning! And encouraging the lads to misbehave; well, I lost a pane of glass, which Tobias will pay for. We've never had that sort of trouble in the village, and I hope I don't live to see the day. I'm surprised the constable let them get away with it!"

Harry had seen him, off duty, enjoying himself; he said nothing, however. Margaret joined them. Rupert kept a hand on her arm until Mrs. Shrewberry had trotted out of earshot, in the complete shelter of her bright green fisherman's umbrella.

"Go ahead, both of you, will you?" he said then. "I'll see you later at the house. I must find out why nobody turned up last night. I'm beginning to feel as if I've got the plague."

Margaret looked skeptical, but she did not argue. She went with Harry to the car. Rupert glanced at his watch. The opening of the Nag's Head coincided with the end of matins, and he guessed he would find most of the men there. He crossed the square with a determined stride. The rain soaked darker patches on his fair hair, and on the shoulders of his jacket.

Rupert was not a drinking man, and he rarely entered the pub. As soon as he came in there was silence. He was surprised to see Mr. Bogle at a corner table, who greeted him with a guarded wave. Mat Shrewberry made a show of being busy behind the bar with glasses and a cloth. Rupert ordered a beer. He had the sense not to begin by buying drinks for everyone in the place.

The room was small, with a low ceiling, and yellowish paint in need of a wash. The fireplace was boarded up; there was a tin stove in the corner whose fumes mixed thickly with the smell of beer and cheap tobacco. The floor was uneven from the idling of generations of boots. Some advertisements for local shows, seasons old, were peeling off the walls.

There were about a dozen men in the room, sitting on benches round the tables or crowding the window seat from which they had a limited view uphill toward the square. Rackstraw was playing a solitary game of darts, an eight-day growth of beard making him look very villainous. Rupert had good aim, but he did not like to barge in and join him. He stood at the bar in the grinding silence. "A filthy day," he made himself remark.

"It is indeed," Mr. Bogle agreed politely. "But seasonable, seasonable."

Mat glanced across the room. He had a bee in his bonnet this morning; he avoided Rupert's eyes, and his clamped lips discouraged talk. In the yellow light of the bar he looked like a sick baby.

Nobody was staring at Rupert, yet he felt as though holes were being bored into his country tweed. He had no wish to finish his pint, and they would think him a fool if he didn't. He pretended to be absorbed in reading the labels on the bottles backing the bar. The atmosphere of the room was such, he could feel his heart beating hard under the hollow of his throat.

"Tellun the mill's for sale," Welsh said, breaking the silence.

Rupert turned his head. "Tellun" was the local word for a rumor.

"Tellun you're after it, Mr. Musgrave." Welsh was enjoying the attention of everyone in the room. He was strongly placed in the darkest corner, between Rackstraw and Mr. Bogle.

"Yes," said Rupert. "That's what I wanted to talk to you about last night." It struck him that he had been naïve to come here and lay himself open to heckling, when he might have guessed that public opinion was building against him. But he was used to thinking of all these men as his friends.

"What will you put in your mill, Mr. Musgrave?" asked the little man eagerly. Mr. Bogle, his eyelids lowered, was rubbing up his spectacles. Everyone else gazed into space, savoring the beer that had to last. Every so often came the *thump* of Rackstraw's darts.

"It'll be fitted with modern machinery."

"Who will you get to work your machines, Mr. Musgrave?" Welsh was making a nonsense of the project with his teasing, singsong voice.

"There'll be work for anyone who wants it," said Rupert shortly. And he was conscious of a stiffening, a prickling through the room, though the slack attitudes of the men did not alter.

"We don't take work from strangers," Welsh announced triumphantly. The question and answer routine had been leading up to this.

"You're a stranger yourself, don't forget!" Rupert angrily retorted. Welsh had come from the mining country when his pit was closed.

Tobias looked in with a message, and Mat left the bar. A couple of men moved up to draw themselves more beer. Rupert said, "Won't you join me?" and put his hand to his pocket. They did not answer, or look at him; only one of them placed the exact change into an ashtray on the counter. In the cramped space they were as close to Rupert as they could be without touching him. He could spy out the pretense of their dress, the places their wives had darned and patched; even the line, which a tie would have hidden, where their necks turned from brown to white. But without saying a word they made it clear that they did not want jobs and wages, or even a drink, from him.

Rupert finished his beer and put down his glass. "It would be steady work," he said. Nobody spoke. "Your wives might thank me," he suggested to the company at large.

Mr. Bogle caught his eye then, and very slightly shook his head as if to warn him that the remark had been a mistake. Rackstraw loomed forward a pace, balancing a dart in his right hand. He had sold his land for a fair price, but he would never forgive Rupert for buying it. "What have our wives got to do with it?" he demanded roughly. "You leave our wives out of this!"

Rupert walked out. He wanted to hurry, but he made himself hold onto his dignity, though it took all the self-control he had. He heard the talk bulge out behind his back, certainly about himself, though he could not distinguish the words. When he reached his car he glanced at himself in the driving mirror before he started the engine. He needed the comfort of an unsurprising face.

He was lunching at Fury Wood. He had to pass the Nag's Head, where he saw Mr. Bogle waiting, bareheaded in the rain, opposite the pub on his side of the road. He pulled up, and opened the passenger door.

"Do you want a lift?"

Mr. Bogle clambered in with fulsome thanks. Doubled into the front seat, he was in danger of scraping his skinny shins against the dashboard.

"I made a pretty good fool of myself, didn't I?" said Rupert, driving on. "I'd give a lot to know why they've suddenly decided I'm a stranger and an enemy. I'd be grateful for a friendly hint."

His companion spread his hands in a deprecatory gesture. "I wish I could enlighten you; but there, I am a newcomer myself."

Rupert glanced at him. "They don't treat you as one!"

At this a particularly bland, even smug smile split the tutor's countenance, that might have irked Rupert if he had happened to see it. "Ah, but I'm such a plain, ordinary person. There's no reason why the least of them should feel at a disadvantage with me," he explained.

"If they've talked to you, I wish you'd pass on the message," persisted Rupert. "You said you were a witch-hunter. Well, I want to know why I'm getting the cold shoulder all of a sudden."

Mr. Bogle sighed. He applied his mind with reluctance to Rupert's problems.

"Try to see it from their point of view. A rich, energetic young man comes along, and wants to take over the village. Of course people feel resentful. It's human nature."

Rupert frowned. He was often baffled by human nature. "Take over!" he repeated. "Heaven knows there are safer investments than that antique mill. Don't you understand, I want to help!"

"No one who knows you could doubt that for a moment," Mr. Bogle assured him. "Your motives are of the highest. Nevertheless these grudges can go very deep; they can even take violent forms. You love the village," he stretched the corners of his smile. "The last thing you want is trouble in Cormundy."

"The last thing I want is to have to uproot myself," said the young man, changing gear for the turn and driving more slowly under the trees. "But if that's got to happen it had better be now than later. I don't want to be ruined, either."

It was strange, the satisfaction that idea seemed to give Mr. Bogle; but he had rearranged his face into a regretful expression by the time they got out of the car and entered the house together.

The discussion continued during lunch. Margaret was optimistic. "Country people hate anything new. They'll come round in time; their wives are already on your side. Oh, ignore the whole thing! It'll blow over."

Mr. Bogle shook his head. "My dear, a mill can't be run without labor. And these men have the habit of idleness." The phrase pleased him; he repeated it, with a mental note to enlarge upon it in his diary. He went on, "If the men won't work, the venture will fail. This fact has to be faced."

"Well, it isn't my mill, so it's not for me to decide," said Margaret with relief, helping them all to a sloppy pudding.

"That's the whole point," said Rupert. "It's not my mill either—yet. I haven't signed the contract. What shall I do—let it go through, and hope for the best, or pull out now before it's too late?"

"What would your father do?" Harry asked abruptly.

"Dad? Oh, he's a fighter. He'd be all for sticking it out, come what may."

"I agree with him," said Harry. "I don't think you can back down just because of a bit of opposition. There's more than your money at stake. You can't expect everyone to cheer you all the time."

There was a silence, broken by Margaret. "That might have been better put."

"Sorry," said Harry. "Excuse me, will you?" He shoved back his chair and limped out of the room.

"All right," said Rupert. "Harry as usual hits the nail on the head. If you both think my reputation is worth such a risk, that settles it."

"Excelsior!" cried Mr. Bogle, with a flourish of his fruit knife. He paused, then added, "About Harry," and he could not help speaking the name as though it had a taste he disliked; he disguised his feelings with a cough, and swallowed some water. "About Harry: does he ever see the doctor? He looks rather pale, and complains of headaches. I have some slight knowledge of medical matters," he informed them, smiling round reassuringly. "A period of rest in a convalescent home might be just what he needs."

"He's not ill," said Margaret at once.

"Not ill, no, no, of course not; but don't you think it might ease him through this difficult period if you asked the doctor to put him into a nursing home, perhaps just until Christmas?" He drew his chair closer to Margaret's; he could see she was troubled. "I feel for poor Harry," he confided. "However much he wants your happiness, it's a wrench, leaving his old home. He's a brave lad, but his heart must ache at times."

Rupert moved quickly to Margaret and put his arms round her. "Oh, don't look so miserable, darling! You must admit Harry's been a bit edgy lately, and we want him right for our wedding, don't we?"

Mr. Bogle smiled and nodded at them both, and tiptoed creakingly away. Once out of sight, however, he glided upstairs with surprising speed. He passed his own room and continued down the passage, still on his toes but so lightly and silently, his feet might have been actually off the ground. He stopped at Harry's door. It was not closed; Harry was sitting reading on the hearthrug, facing the fire. If he had turned his head he would have seen Mr. Bogle, who hovered there for several minutes, staring in at him with the most poisonous expression.

The next day, Rupert drove into town and signed the contract for the mill, and the battle over Cormundy entered its second phase.

A few hours after the mill changed hands, Mr. Bogle set off on foot to the village with one of his surprise suitcases. It was evening. A drizzly rain would clear as the night got colder, but by the time he had climbed the hill to the pub, the whole surface of his head was damp and shiny. He did not go into the bar; he made his way round by the back to the skittle alley. He was expected there, though no game was in progress. He dived in with smiles and greetings.

His friends had multiplied since the meeting at Fury Wood, but they did not seem to have gained in self-confidence. They were listening a little regretfully to the cheerful hum coming from the bar next door. Mr. Bogle opened his case, keeping up a peddler's patter, and began piecing together a battered black projector, while he sent a man down the alley to hang a sheet across the far wall where the skittles were stuck up. The rest watched these preparations without much enthusiasm. They had been promised a film show, but evidently it was going to be an amateur performance.

Mr. Bogle placed the projector squarely on a table, and turned to a box of filmstrips through which his long fingers rapidly flickered. "Aha, this is the one I'd earmarked for you! *Memory Lane*, it's called. Of course, it may not be what you want—it may not fit the bill; well, then we'll try another. There are plenty to choose from."

The alley was plunged into darkness as he fumbled for a connection. In a few moments a square of speckled light appeared, and he began turning the handle of the machine. His audience stared at the screen with awakened interest. The maker's sign came first—three triangles laid across to form a star; it was followed in jerks by a fuzzy view. Mr. Bogle adjusted the lens, apologizing for the quality of the picture. "It was made some years ago. But we all know where we are. We approach Cormundy . . . there's the church. Dear old place. . . . That's the old covered market in the square; people used to come from miles around to buy and sell there. And the old school . . . remember the horseshoes and hopscotch, and a week off from lessons at haymaking time? Are your own kiddies any better for their posh education? It'll take them away from you in the end, away from the village. . . . But that's progress, I suppose."

The airplane or broomstick, or whatever it was that carried the camera, lost height to hover over the smallholdings that used to exist in the country round the hill, homely old farms with gardens and duck ponds and orchards. The men were touched by childhood scenes.

"There's Bert Rackstraw's place!" someone exclaimed. "It was a fair farm, Bert, in those days!"

Rackstraw bit his bristly lip, as the camera lingered over his wound. "It was the cattle brought us down," he muttered.

"Tellun young Musgrave is fetching in bullocks next month," rumbled Titmuss.

"I hope they may do the same to him!"

Rackstraw was not alone with his grievance; the film roused general resentment. Mr. Bogle knew which villagers were his friends, and how to bind them. When it finished, he had the sequel ready; while he fitted it into the projector he listened to the glum voices. "What could I do? There was the wife and kids to consider." "The price seemed fair, at the time." "We all know who's profited on the deal!"

"This film is only six months old," said Mr. Bogle. "It won't tell you anything you don't already know, only too well. The land taken over by Musgrave has been thickly outlined. I don't have to remind you that he's increased his property since."

But their memories had been stirred, and the changes struck freshly to the heart of everyone there. The orchards, the gardens and lanes where they had played as children and later walked with their sweethearts had all been swept away. Bought up, the small holders had retreated to the hill, and their loss had been the death of Cormundy. The market and school had gone, with the annual show, the smithy and bakery and saddler's. Now all supplies had to come from the town. There were the summer visitors, of course. "The average tourist spends about fifty pence when he visits Cormundy," Mr. Bogle remarked. Everyone knew that this was true. One could do the church and have a slap-up tea at Mrs. Shrewberry's for less than that.

Rupert was the only big landowner to live near the village, and judging by the line marking his boundaries, he was responsible for a third of the devastating corn. The ingenious cameraman had invaded his farm; his shining equipment was shown in detail, his great barns, his harvester which did the work of a team of men. The film ended there, but it left a clear target. It seemed to justify the hard feelings that had been brewing against Rupert; everyone was angry, while Welsh, who alone had lost nothing, denounced him the loudest of all.

The packed alley was dreadfully hot, for there were no windows, and no one made a move to open the door. A canopy of tobacco smoke floated overhead, opaque in the beam of the projector. By now they were all of one mind, any personal grudges among them forgotten; but

Mr. Bogle did not interrupt the clamor, or suggest a plan of action. Tonight it sufficed to have won their undivided attention; and sure enough, as he wound in the third and last strip, everyone fell silent and turned eagerly toward the screen.

It was Cormundy, but not the village they knew. A rough stone church towered over a cluster of medieval huts. The plain all round was thickly covered with trees. The film had the brownish tinge of old photography, which gave the scene a menacing effect, while the heavy outlines looked as if they had been singed into it. The constant flickering of the projector added to this *burnt* impression.

A shadow rose across the screen, out of focus, as if Mr. Bogle was being careless and getting his hand in the light. And a line of men came creeping out of the forest, up the hill. They did not look like men at first, because they had horns; but they walked erect. They were carrying poles with smoking ends. The roof of the nearest hut began to waver and smoke.

The hearts of the watchers in the skittle alley were beating hard. Somebody swore in a low voice when the cigarette he had forgotten burnt his fingers; no one took his eyes for one second off the picture. Now the horned men had disappeared, but the huts were smoking, and pale fire belched from the door of the church. Then the intermediate shadow spread, deepened, until it entirely swallowed the little scene.

Nobody spoke. Mr. Bogle went on winding his ancient projector. They were looking again at Cormundy. The huts had been replaced by mud and wattle buildings, some of which still survived; the church was recognizably their own with its spire and flying buttresses. The sky was a dingier brown; evidently it was evening. A broad track led across country, where much of the forest had been cleared. A company of mounted soldiers was approaching the village, riding at ease, perhaps intending to put up there for the night.

And again the shadow pushed up the picture.

The soldiers reached the incline of the hill, dropped the reins on the horses' necks to let them pick their way, disappeared one by one between the houses. All was still. Then a thread of smoke spiraled up, and another; there followed bursts of colorless flame. A riderless horse careered downhill with flapping stirrups, fleeing panic-stricken into the trees; after it streamed men brandishing sticks and torches. Perhaps they caught even that last horse, but the picture darkened as they entered the wood.

"Cromwell's men were unpopular in Cormundy," Mr. Bogle observed. "They made the mistake of burning Fury Wood. But after this—happening—they left the village in peace."

Now for the last time the hill lay before them, unbuilt, bald as a bell between the treeless earth, the cloudless sky. A party of men was loping back from the foreground—from the alley itself, it seemed. And the watchers caught their breath, as each of them thought he recognized himself. They stared anxiously at their own purposeful back views. But this company did not climb the hill. As soon as they reached it they disappeared, within it or into thin air, until there was nothing left but that brown landscape of terrible simplicity.

Then the hill began to lose its density. It became smoky, penetrable; and in the very middle of it, deeply buried, there was a pair of eyes.

The hill writhed, and wreathed, dissolving in smoke. The eyes grew steadily sharper, as if they were approaching. The smoke drifted off the screen and hung in the beam of the projector, continuing its incessant, inward movement, within the vague outline of an antlered head. The eyes advanced with it in the room.

There was no sound in the alley, not a whisper. Twenty men stood spellbound there, and you could have heard a pin drop.

Mr. Bogle switched off. "Good night!" he said. "I hope you've enjoyed your evening. One moment, let me get the door open." For the men were like sleepwalkers, stumbling about. They had lost all sense of time. The church clock striking eleven across the square was an astonishment.

The doorway was narrow; they had to file past Mr. Bogle. Going out, each man felt a fleeting touch on the cheek, a light scrape like the brush of a fly.

5

Dr. Spencer-Venables was a breezy townsman, anxious to dispel the mysteries surrounding his craft. With this end in view, he was casual with his instruments, and kept up a bracing conversation with Margaret about Christmas and the weather, as though she was the person he had come to see. On the side, in brackets so to speak, he listened to Harry's chest, took his blood pressure, and examined his legs. At the end he tossed his things back into his case with relief, as if they were a disreputable secret he liked to conceal. Harry waited for the verdict. All his bones felt at their softest.

"You're doing fine," said the doctor. He looked at Harry and grinned. "You don't believe me, do you? All the same, one of these days you're going to astonish yourself. You're going to find you can run!"

Harry was speechless. He furtively wriggled his toes.

"Try to imagine those muscles and nerves like broken electric wires. Now you may not know it, but they're growing stronger all the time, and when they make contact—bingo! A couple of pains, and you're home!"

This was his way of preparing one for a difficult climax, as Margaret would discover next year when Rupert's son was being born.

"That's marvelous!" she said.

"He ought to take as much exercise as he can," said jolly Spencer-Venables, poised for departure. "There's nothing like fresh air. We'll keep him back from school until next term."

"He does lessons here," said Margaret. "As a matter of fact it was his tutor who advised me to call you."

Harry looked up sharply. "You didn't tell me that!"

But they continued their conversation as if he were invisible.

"You aren't driving straight back into town, by any chance?" she asked.

"Yes, why? Do you want a lift?"

"I would be grateful. The car was serviced today, and there's no bus until evening. Of course the garage is shut by then."

"Always ready to oblige," he joked, and to Harry, "So long, chum. Remember what one snail said to the other, keep moving." And he went away, banging and whistling like a milkman.

"You'll be all right, won't you?" said Margaret hurriedly. "No more work today, Mr. Bogle went out after lunch. If Rupert calls, tell him where I am. But I won't be long." She bent forward quickly and kissed him. "I'm so glad you're better," she said. And she ran down the passage to catch the doctor.

It was dreary weather, but just then the sun nudged whitely through the clouds. It drew the glow from the fire, and made the room seem colder. Harry shivered. He did not feel in the least like taking any health-giving exercise. He got up and limped to the shelves to choose a book.

And his hand fell at once on one he had never seen before. It was plainly bound in brown cloth. He stared at it, surprised; pulled it out, and opened it. There was the Longshaw coat of arms on the flyleaf. But he was quite certain that it did not belong to him; and sure enough it had no number, although he had made an index of every book in the library. The paper was thick and unevenly cut, with the horizontal grain of pretentious stationery, and reminded him at once of Mr. Bogle. Harry loved books, but even his fingertips distrusted this one.

He turned a page. *Cernunnos Hys Galantie Showe*, he read—that was all; no author, no publisher, no date.

And no story: the book contained a series of murky brown photographs touched up by hand to resemble pastel drawings. The subject was a man, dressed in a flapping animal skin and crowned with antlers. Each page showed him in a slightly different attitude.

Harry took the book to the window sill, and resting it there, looked through the pictures. They were stylized, almost coy; the model had been given a woodsy make-up, suggestive of nymphs and fauns. But there was something uncommonly sinister behind this dated rubbish. *Galantie Showe*—what was that? Harry began to find it difficult to breathe. He went on staring at the pictures because more and more he dreaded that if he moved or turned his head in the least degree, he would discover Cernunnos, a horned reality, behind him at the door. His heart, battling with this terror, pounded against his ribs like a frog hammer.

The pigeon flew up to the window, making him jump so that he lost his grip of the pages. They flickered under his gaze, the poses of the cloaked figure merging into a rapid dance before the book snapped shut. Harry let in the bird with a trembling hand. Then he opened the book again and loosed the pages evenly. The figure pranced and leapt. It was an ingenious way of giving a dancing lesson. Harry's face was perfectly white. His spine shrank from his clammy shirt.

He would have thrown it on the fire at once, but he had the uncanny feeling that it might explode. He could not have explained why it repelled him. The pictures were not obscene. Indeed, many people might find them interesting and unusual; it was easy to imagine their kind faces bending over that book. Even Margaret's, and he knew he had to get rid of it. He decided to wrap it in newspaper and put it in the garbage can.

He limped along the landing. His progress was considerably hindered by the book, which was heavier than it looked and had a tendency to slip backward under his arm so that he nearly dropped it several times, and he needed both hands for the stairs. Halfway down, it fell over the banisters and onto the hall floor with a crash. He got on more quickly without it. When he rounded the stairs, he saw that it was lying open. It struck him then that there was something familiar about the figure straddling the page. He could not place that dancing man; and yet the thought nagged him.

He picked it up gingerly and went to the kitchen where old newspapers were kept. A reek of Mrs. Gallops, vegetables that had boiled dry, steamed cod, and tepid fat, hit him when he opened the door. She had gone home, but the room was being used by several cats who were balancing on the ledges of windows and cupboards, and crouching in the spatter of ash before the stove. He did not know they owned so many. A row of washed stockings hung across the chimney, as if it was already Christmas Eve; Mrs. Gallops' apron, widely spread, gave an indication of her bulk.

Harry made a parcel of *Cernunnos Hys Galantie Showe*, and opened the back door. The garbage cans stood near at the edge of the wood. A couple of rats who had been scouring a tin shuffled off at the sight of him. He dumped the book, and walked on round the back. This was the part he had played in most as a child; a hiding place he had made still hung overhead like a rotting nest. But neither he nor Margaret would miss the house.

He reached the corner, the stables where logs were chopped. The wind blew keenly up the gap in the woods, which held a stillness, a winter breathlessness. The shadows of the trees lay like black rays all pointing toward the house. Harry wished he had Tobias with him. He would have given a lot to see Rupert riding up the drive, scattering any horned figures that might be lurking behind the trees. He limped on as briskly as he could.

Then he stopped dead, listened, raised his eyes to the branches.

The rooks had gone.

Harry's heart sank. He stared in dismay at the rookery littering the top boughs of the elms, as if he could see the luck of the house falling away.

The woods had a trampled look. They had the sad coloring of mourning, the quietness of death.

He decided to telephone Rupert. As he let himself back in, he caught a glimpse of his own face in the sliver of mirror set into the hat and coat stand, and he noted with a flash of illogical satisfaction that in spite of the doctor's vaunted fresh air, he looked paler than ever. He sat on the bottom stair and dialed Rupert's number, and then he wondered what on earth he was going to say. He did not want to talk about *Cernunnos Hys Galantie Showe,* and Rupert would think it odd of him to worry about the birds.

All this time the phone was ringing, and Rupert did not answer. After a few minutes Harry replaced the receiver. The thought of hearing Rupert had given him strength. Now the darkness around the house seemed to be seeping inside.

He looked at his watch. It would be half an hour at least before Margaret came in, and she might easily remember something she had to do at the farm first. He decided to go back to his room and draw. It was the best way he knew of passing the time.

When he reached Mr. Bogle's door, he noticed that it was slightly ajar. That was a sure sign that he was still out; he had a way of softly shutting himself inside that made itself felt through the house. Harry hesitated on the landing. He could not see far into the room beyond a corner of the bed curtains. Presently, overcome by curiosity, he pushed the door a little wider and peered cautiously inside.

Mr. Bogle had been playing some kind of game at his desk. Harry limped forward to look. Mr. Bogle was evidently a genius with paper models; he had made a little scene with the church, Fury Wood, Rupert's farm and the mill. Harry stared down at the toys, completely mystified.

There was room on the desk for Mr. Bogle's diary. It was open, and his spectacles lay on top of it. Now Harry might have wondered how far he could have gone without them; but he was distracted by a glimpse through the lens. Although the diary appeared to be in code, the thick glass made it legible simply by magnifying the writing to normal size. A sentence caught his eye: "Harry has a high opinion of his own ability." He blushed angrily, and pushed the glasses farther up the page. "Harry lacks application," he could not help reading, and, "I think Harry can never amount to much."

But then, like a slow tide freezing his blood, there crept over him again that terrible feeling that somebody, something was behind him. He pressed against the desk. He could not believe that Mr. Bogle, who was as clumsy as an elephant, could have come upstairs unheard. All the same, the conviction that he was being watched grew until he could no longer bear it. He swallowed hard, and turning his head very slightly, he looked round out of the corners of his eyes.

Mr. Bogle had been in the room all the time. He was lying on his bed with his eyes open, and his mouth stretched in a dark grin.

That night was bitter in Cormundy. The clanking church clock seemed to thin the air, and hone the edge of the frost. The very tombstones quailed under it; and it struck upon the head of the old tramp picking his way among them, as if to warn him that his time was nearly up.

He was carrying a billycan and a kerosene stove, and was making his way across the churchyard to boil up a nightcap in the lee of the wall. It was the most sheltered corner, and there was a soft bit of compost to sit on while he waited for his tea. He squatted, and put a match to the stove. When he had spent an evening at the Nag's Head, the tombstones looked rockier than ever. They were his companions of the night. "What's this, Emma?" he muttered, leering at *Emma Rix, departed this life aged seventy-five, a dutiful wife,* who was reeling at an angle of sixty degrees. "You've been at the bottle again, haven't you? Naughty girl!"

A black figure loomed behind the stone. The tramp backed, gibbering, glaring through the light of his little fire until he upset the pan steaming on it and put it out.

"Don't you come any nearer!" he croaked, his voice grating like a rusty lock. "I'll call the constable! Assaulting a harmless old man, that's what you are, and there's a law against it!"

The ghost moved calmly toward him, set up the stove and struck a match. The face overhanging the flame was then revealed as Mr. Bogle's.

"Come, come, pull yourself together. You know me," he said irritably.

The old man quieted, but he stared at his visitor with the greatest suspicion. "What are you doing here, at this time of night?" he growled at last.

"I've come to see you, that's obvious, isn't it?" Mr. Bogle took no trouble to sound agreeable. The tramp reeked of the pub. "Come closer, you silly old fool, right up to the stove. I'd have talked to you during the day, wouldn't I, if I'd wanted to be overheard?"

The tramp shuffled forward reluctantly, and stretched his hands to the fire. He was wearing holey mittens, somebody's cast-offs. The heat seemed to reassure him, and he looked pityingly at his knotted fingers while from time to time he cast stealthy glances in the direction of his companion, whom he knew to be crouching opposite, beyond the glow of the stove.

"You used to make scarecrows, didn't you?" Mr. Bogle demanded abruptly.

"Nobody wants them now. Come spring they set up automatic bangers, like guns going off in your ear. Where's the art in that?" said the old man, searching the darkness with his bleary eyes for a sympathetic response.

"I want six. I'll pay you a pound apiece, and no gabbing."

The tramp's jaw dropped. "A pound apiece?" His croak mounted to a squeak. "Six quid? What'll I do for straw?"

"I've already seen to that. Well, take it or leave it."

"Take it!" And he wiped the back of a mitten across his mouth, relishing the future.

"No gabbing, remember," Mr. Bogle repeated warningly. "One word—just one—and I'll cleave your tongue to the roof of your mouth, and smother you with black scab."

"Don't talk like that," said the tramp, shifting uneasily. "I don't think it's funny."

"I've got more than jokes up my sleeve, I promise

you. Where will you work? You mustn't be seen."

The tramp thought for a minute. "The crypt. That's where I sleep, this time of year. Nobody goes down there, nobody can. I keep it locked."

"The crypt," agreed Mr. Bogle. "Very good. Now about the dolls—I mean, scarecrows. I want you to bind one of these articles inside each. Hold out your hand."

The tramp hesitated, doubting what he might receive. He could hear Mr. Bogle feeling through his pockets with a rustling sound. "I daresay," he ventured in a wheedling tone, "you'd thought of paying a small advance, on account? I'd work the quicker for it."

"Not a penny," said Mr. Bogle emphatically. "There's no hurry. You'll have them ready by Christmas. Here, take these things. Come on, man, they won't bite you!"

He handed over a pen, a handkerchief, a sock, a comb, and two pieces of paper. "Personal belongings, bits of trash, easier to collect than clippings of hair or nails, and just as powerful. Don't forget," he said, and his voice was somber, "I want one bound into each figure. *And no gabbing.*"

The tramp raised his eyes. Mr. Bogle was steadily regarding him over the hissing flame. Next moment he had disappeared into the darkness.

The tramp shivered. He turned over the articles in his fingers. The handkerchief was made of fine linen, embroidered with the initial *R.* He envied the gray woolen sock, and might have changed it for one of the holey pair on his own feet, but he was afraid of Mr. Bogle. He unfolded the first piece of paper. It was a letter from Rupert to Mr. Bogle, confirming the details of his employment at Fury Wood. The tramp held it as close to the flame as he could without setting it alight, and tried to puzzle it out, his hoarse breath mingling with the fumes of the stove.

He opened the second paper. There were six words scrawled across it in untidy capitals: EXORIARE ALIQUIS NOSTRIS EX OSSIBUS ULTOR. They made no sense to him. Staring stupidly at them, he thought he saw a pattern in the paper, antlers, and something like a face.

The churchyard was making him jumpy. It was too bad that he had nowhere else to go on a night like this; his mouth drooped with self-pity. He extinguished his stove, and stuffing everything into the huge pockets of the coat he always wore, he set off, crunching across the frosty churchyard.

He paused at the head of the steps leading down to the crypt. It had occurred to him that Mr. Bogle's feet had made no sound, no sound at all, though the grass crackled like paper and the night was as clear as a bell.

6

"Does *Cernunnos Hys Galantie Showe* mean anything to you?" Harry asked Margaret next time they were alone together.

"No. Should it?"

He described the book. He avoided her eyes while he talked about it; he was unable to convey its effect, and he knew that to her it was nothing significant. "Horns and dancing?" she said vaguely when he had finished. "It sounds like Mr. Bogle."

"Exactly," said Harry, concentrating on his egg—it was breakfast, and she was sitting on the end of his bed. "But why should he go to the trouble of sticking one of our bookplates into it, and planting it in here?"

"You've been reading too many thrillers." She opened the window for the pigeon and it hobbled inside, disdaining to use its wings which were pinkly tinged with the rosy, frosty sky. It got onto the rim of the tray and pecked at the bread and butter. "He knows you like old books. I expect he meant it for a present."

"Joke," said Harry, spreading marmalade. He wanted to tell her what he had read in Mr. Bogle's diary, but he felt ashamed of having spied.

"He's got a kind heart," Margaret insisted. "He paid for all that beer on Guy Fawkes Day, Mat's wife told me. And he can't resist a stray cat; the kitchen's full of them."

"Oh, those are the Bogle's cats, are they?" said Harry with his mouth full. "I don't know why you call it kind. Haven't you seen his fur dressing gown?"

"Don't be horrid!" Then Margaret began to laugh. "He's begun wearing it at breakfast since the weather got colder. It certainly is a hideous garment. And isn't he getting fat! I'm sure he wasn't that size when he came. He's put on at least fifteen pounds. I must stop," she said. "It's mean to mock him, when he's so nice about all of us. And he thinks a friend of his may be interested in buying the house, for some sort of youth work."

"But we don't want his friends here!" exclaimed Harry, frowning.

"Don't be ridiculous, beggars can't be choosers! We'll be lucky if anyone buys it."

"No wonder the rooks have cleared off."

"I've asked him to my wedding, by the way," said

Margaret, studying her engagement ring.

"Who? The Bogle, or his rich friend?"

"Mr. Bogle, of course. You needn't be sarcastic. He was awfully pleased. It'll give him a chance to show off his dancing. And now I'm going to try on my wedding dress, and you can tell me how I look in it."

There was no connecting door between his room and hers; she had to go all the way round by the passage. He sat in bed and waited. The cobwebs across the outside of his window looked like frozen rigging. He gazed down the wood, where a fine day was gradually asserting itself. Even the empty nests seemed less of an omen.

He heard Margaret coming, the rustle of her dress. He watched the door expectantly, but he was not prepared, not in the least, for the look of her.

"Don't you like it?" she asked a little anxiously, when he didn't speak.

"Oh yes," he said. "You look beautiful."

The dress was very simple, long, and close-fitting to the waist, cut low to show the soft set of Margaret's neck. The bodice and sleeves were edged with lace; there was no other trimming. The green-sprigged cotton was wonderfully light and radiant. Harry said, "You look like a May Queen."

"I'm going to carry white freesias, and wear them in my hair. Rupert's growing them specially. We're decorating the church out of his greenhouse, all white, because of Christmas. White chrysanthemums, and more freesias on the altar."

Then they heard somebody coming along the passage.

"Oh!" exclaimed Margaret. "If that's Rupert, he mustn't see me!"

"Don't worry," said Harry. "That's not Rupert, he doesn't flounder along like that."

All the same Margaret hid behind the door. But when Mr. Bogle came in, she stepped forward. "Harry's not up yet, and it's my fault, I'm afraid."

Mr. Bogle took one look at her, and his sallow complexion turned gray. Still staring, he backed out of the room. He shut the door quietly behind him, and they heard him plunging away.

Margaret looked guiltily at Harry. "I suppose he thought I was in my nightgown!"

"He's probably never seen one before. It's been a nasty shock. Hooray," said Harry, stretching, and moving farther down the bed. "He'll need the morning off to recover."

"Indeed he won't! You must get up, and if he still looks upset you'd better say something casual; you could ask him how he liked my *wedding dress*."

"Who cares? It's not him you're marrying."

Margaret lingered by the bed in a reflective silence. Harry looked her over once more, and suffered a twinge of pain. She liked to assure him that marriage would not change her, but of course it would; women belonged to their husbands, not their brothers. It hurt to remember that their time alone together was running out. He asked abruptly, "What are you thinking about?"

"Rupert phoned this morning. Somebody broke into the mill; he's got to put in a guard dog."

"Did they do any harm?"

"Not much: the new machinery hasn't been put in yet. They forced a lock which needed replacing anyway, and scribbled a few rude messages on the walls."

"*Capitalists go home.*"

"That sort of thing. And he had some bales of straw pinched from the farm. It doesn't amount to a lot in terms of cash, but he hates the feeling that people are against him."

"Has he told the police?"

"Good heavens, no! He thinks the less he makes of it, the easier it'll be to forget when it all blows over. And that's true, of course."

"He was always the blue-eyed boy of the wives and mothers," Harry remarked, reaching for his clothes.

"He still is, thank goodness. They're the only ray of hope at the moment. It's funny, isn't it, how people suddenly turn? They're jealous I suppose."

"Maybe the Bogle was right."

"How do you mean?"

"Maybe there are witches in Cormundy. It's a mistake to hunt them. It wakes them up."

Mr. Bogle had his nose to the grindstone by the time Harry joined him downstairs. The stouter he grew, the more his shadow spread about him. It already extended to the middle of the carpet; languidly setting out his books, Harry calculated how much more he would have to swell before he engulfed the whole room.

Mrs. Gallops bounded in with two parcels, scattering Mr. Bogle's correspondence. One had come for him through the post; the other, on which Harry's eyes at once riveted, was thickly wrapped in newspaper.

Mr. Bogle scrabbled with his left hand for the letters that had fallen to the floor. His right hand rested on the newspaper parcel.

Mrs. Gallops went away. Harry pretended to be engrossed in his exercise; after a few minutes he glanced casually across the table. Mr. Bogle had unwrapped *Cernunnos Hys Galantie Showe*. He was absorbed in the pictures and did not raise his head, but asked at once, "Why did you throw this away?"

Harry stared at him.

"I was watching you yesterday, from my window. I wondered what you were up to, so I asked Mrs. Gallops to investigate. Oh, I don't mind telling you all this! I like to be open and aboveboard with everybody."

Harry felt the guilty color rising in his cheeks.

"I wonder how you'd feel if you caught me reading your private diary," Mr. Bogle pensively remarked.

"It was all about me, anyhow," Harry said, rallying to defend himself.

"All about *you*?" Mr. Bogle sounded genuinely surprised.

"The bits I read were."

"You amaze me! Do you seriously think I haven't anything more interesting to write about? But come along, I want to know why you threw away the book."

"Because it isn't mine, and I don't want it," said Harry, after a silence. He could feel the claws of a headache deepening in his skull.

"*Not* yours? Surely this is your coat of arms on the flyleaf? *Mon âme, mon epée*," read Mr. Bogle, making it sound pretentious.

"There are spare bookplates in the library. Anyone could have stuck it in."

"Anyone? That's weak, for you. I'm sure you've already thought of a culprit. Mrs. Gallops, perhaps? Even, dare I suggest it, my humble self?"

"All right," and Harry suddenly lost his temper, "why not? Yes, I do think you planted the book; and since we're on the subject, I bet you hung the dummy in the cupboard. It's the same sort of trick."

Mr. Bogle's head remained bent over the table, but at these words he raised his eyes to Harry's. The whites underlined the brown, glinting through his spectacles like a double meaning.

"Very good," he said in a low voice. "No more beating about the bush. Since we know so much about each other, why shouldn't we be friends?"

Harry did not answer. Their arms were nearly touching; he withdrew his, and opened a book.

"One offer of friendship, rejected," murmured the

darkling Bogle. "Your sister should have sent you away, she could have insisted. Well, it's too late now. . . . Dear me," he said in a different tone, "this room is very airless this morning!" And hooking his thumbs into the armholes of his jacket, he shook it to let a draft circulate. "Now, don't you want to see what I've got in my *other* little parcel?"

He made a great performance of opening it, undoing all the knots. Inside, there was a cardboard box held together with rubber bands. He snapped them off, economically rolling them up his shirt cuff, punctuating his unwrapping with a hopeful patter: "I really believe this may be what I've been waiting for! Oh, excitement! Thrill of thrills . . . Can it be? It is!" he triumphantly exclaimed, unfolding the last tissue paper, and gazing down with delight.

Harry looked up. There on the table between them, in a nest of cotton wool, lay a crescent-shaped necklet, about an inch thick all the way round, made of a weightless, glittering alloy. Its two ends were decorated with raised bands of the same metal. It looked like a bit of cheap costume jewelry.

"It's only a copy, of course," Mr. Bogle explained, still poring over his treasure. "It would never do to risk one of the old torques, even if we could get it out of a museum. They were always worn, you know, in the old rituals—but there, it's not a pretty history. All the same I like it, I like it very much. Do you want to try it on?" he rounded on Harry with enthusiasm.

"No, thanks . . . *you* try it," Harry added in an effort to sound less churlish.

"Oh no, I shan't wear it. It's my gift. Well, I'm sorry it's not good enough for you."

It occurred to Harry that the torque might be intended for a wedding present. He lied, "I expect Margaret'll like it."

"This has nothing to do with Margaret," Mr. Bogle told him reprovingly.

When Harry went upstairs he found *Cernunnos Hys Galantie Showe* lying on the bed. He opened the window, and hurled it with all his strength toward the wood. He half expected it to come sailing back at him; but it hit the stable chimney and slid down the roof into the gutter, out of sight.

After this Harry stopped killing time with the exploits of invented snobs. On the contrary, it was Mr. Bogle himself who stretched the bounds of possibility, daily waxing in jollity and fatness. But his shadow always kept pace with him, his dark potential that began to make itself felt, as though the deepening winter had got into the house.

There came days when Harry could hardly bring himself to enter the room they shared, or raise his eyes to the face across the table. Mr. Bogle had large features, but they were oddly blank—like a pumpkin lantern's before the candle is put inside. Harry dreaded catching him *lit up*.

7

December came, and the last weeks at Fury Wood gathered speed. Two men in overalls stripped the house of all the furniture worth taking to the farm. Harry lost his ancestors; they were carried off one by one, looking with calm faces over the shoulders of the moving men. His corner cupboard went, too, and he put his mice into Margaret's old dollhouse. They seemed to enjoy the change.

Now the house knew it was beaten, and no longer made any attempt to keep up appearances. The paler squares left by pictures and furniture showed up like scars in the rooms.

Mr. Bogle grew sentimental as Christmas drew near, indulging in throwaway remarks such as: "Sad to think our paths must soon diverge, never, who knows, to cross again!" and: "It is but seldom, in the race of life, that we run the whole course with our friends." It sounded as if he was already composing letters to write to them. He took to playing his violin if he was alone in the evening; the notes quivered in the chilly atmosphere like the plaint of the melancholy house. But this line in gothic romance hung oddly on his new corpulence. Even Margaret thought he was overdoing it.

In Cormundy all the loafers turned out to watch the Longshaw possessions being moved to the Musgrave farm. The road was too steep and narrow for the van, which was in difficulties from one end of the hill to the other. But nobody offered to help. A day or two later, a cattle truck ground through at a walking pace, with Rupert's bullocks in it. Mrs. Shrewberry's willow pattern got the jitters in the dresser. The bullocks threw back their heads and stared between the slats of the truck with rolling eyes. The driver wanted to know the way; he was a stranger there. But the men he questioned turned silently away. He was lucky to meet Tobias coming home from school, who climbed into the cab as a guide. He found out from him how to avoid the village on the return journey.

On December 23rd, Margaret and Rupert met in the church. Rupert had driven over with the flowers; the head of the nave was knee-deep in potted chrysanthemums, and creaking bunches of winter blossom.

"I've been a fool," he said abruptly.

Margaret stroked his sleeve without speaking. She knew what was coming.

"We should have left. We should have gone away to be married. What if they cut our wedding the way they have the meetings, what if nobody comes? What a waste of time and money!"

"We'll be here, and Harry, and your parents. That's all that matters. But of course people will come," she said, with a glance at him. "The women certainly will. And I don't see the men staying away from a party, even one at the Musgrave farm." She moved a white chrysanthemum to the corner of the communion step, and stood back to gauge the effect.

"How long will you be?" said Rupert.

"Most of the morning. There's the crib to do."

He began walking down the nave. She said, "Where are you going?"

"To try and get some sense into their heads."

"Do you think that's wise?" He did not answer. "What will you say?"

"God knows." He paused and turned. High above his head, the carved roof had a look of struggling. The angels or evangelists supported it, as they had for hundreds of years. Margaret was watching him anxiously, wiping at her hair with one hand.

"I'm sorry," he said. "I used to think I'd be quite a good match for someone. But I don't know that you're getting such a bargain."

"You're all I want."

"That's all right, then." He smiled quickly, nodded, and left the church.

The crib was already in position, at the entrance to the Lady chapel. Margaret had brought evergreens with her from Fury Wood, and now she began fitting them into the frame of the little stable. They were soaked with the rain that had fallen during the night. Her fingers grew cold and red, but she was happy, working there. She knelt to arrange the Holy Family in the straw and put the shepherds round them, with the ox and ass at a respectful distance.

When she got up she draped the stable with a washed-out, purplish cloth, which the vicar would remove when he came into the church on Christmas morning. She bowed as she left the Lady chapel; perhaps because her own mother was dead, she had a devotion to the Queen of Heaven.

Rupert came out into the square. It was very cold. Tobias and some of his friends were standing with their noses pressed to the window of Welsh's shop, watching a cartoon on the television. Rupert hesitated, then crossed and tapped Tobias on the shoulder. "Do me a favor. Go to the Nag's Head and tell the men in the bar that I want to talk to them out here. Tell your brother, too, and anyone else you can find."

Tobias stared at him, shrugged, and sloped off. Rupert walked by the churchyard wall, reading the inscriptions on the tombstones. The grave mounds had distinct, wintry shapes. After a few minutes he could hear people coming into the square, behind his back. He took a grip on himself, and turned and faced them.

"Thanks for coming," he said. "I must say I didn't expect it." He thought his voice sounded weak, and when he spoke again he raised it almost to a shout. "It's cold out here, and I'll come straight to the point. We used to be good friends. I don't know what happened to change it."

Titmuss the butcher came out of his shop and leant against the angle of the window. His expression was stern, and just. He had left the door ajar; inside, his boy was chopping meat on the block.

"I haven't changed," said Rupert. "I still want what I always wanted, to help the village."

"We don't need your help!" somebody shouted from the back. Rupert recognized Rackstraw, with his grizzled beard.

"Okay, so the boot's on the other foot, and I need yours," he returned sharply. "The last bit of machinery goes into the mill today, and I want to start work straight after Christmas. There'll be a decent job for anyone who wants it."

"After Christmas!" shouted Mat, fidgeting about with excitement. "There's a lot can happen between now and Christmas!"

"I'd better make it clear that if there's any more

messing about on my property, I'll prosecute! The dog has the run of the place, so trespassers are likely to be caught."

"What is this, threats?" yelled Rackstraw, whose speech turned guttural when he was excited.

"And there's another thing!" Now Rupert had to shout, to be heard above the crowd. "You signed on as my stockman, Quotter, but you haven't turned up for work yet!"

Peter Quotter grinned sheepishly and nudged his mates.

"Won't catch *him* doing the mucky work!" jeered Welsh, jerking his head at Rupert.

"Who else d'you think's been doing it? You know me better than that! Who's been selling you this pack of lies?"

The crowd caught the pain in his voice, and shifted uneasily. But Rackstraw made a joke of it with a rude noise.

"You can't patch things up this way, Mr. Musgrave," said the deep-voiced Titmuss. "You aren't doing any good."

"I'm not trying to patch things up!" Rupert turned to the butcher, whose solid frame seemed to embody order and good sense. "We're talking about the future of Cormundy. Do you really want to throw it away?"

"Doesn't he talk like the big boss?" cried Mat, waving his arms with his back to Rupert as if he were conducting an orchestra. "But we don't have to listen to his sort anymore. Oh yes, your future is going to catch up with you, Mr. Musgrave! Sooner than you think!"

Rupert heard him with despair as he scanned the crowd. They were not wicked people, but every face was touched with malice. He said, "You know what my plans are, you've known from the beginning. And Margaret and I still hope you'll come to church tomorrow to see us married. Afterward, at the farm, there'll be plenty to eat and drink for everyone."

He turned and walked up the path between the graves. He was afraid that the last sentence had sounded like a bribe, and his enemies would use it against him. When he reached the church porch, he sat down on the bench and discovered that his legs were trembling. The tramp in the corner nodded and smiled. He, too, was beyond the pale. Rupert felt in his pocket, and handed him some money.

Margaret left home after lunch, in a chaos of last-minute packing. There was no room in the car for Harry, or at the farm until after the wedding; Rupert's parents were arriving that night. So he had to stay at Fury Wood with Mr. Bogle. He stood in the doorway to say good-bye. His breath matched the fog thickening the wood.

Margaret climbed into the car and slammed the door. She leaned out of the window.

"I've got your suit and your shoes, so don't worry

about them; and Rupert or someone will get you in good time tomorrow, then you can change with us and we'll all go to church together. Do you think it'll snow? This mist could turn to anything. Don't get cold," she warned him. She started the engine. "So it's good-bye to the old home!"

He waved. As she passed him he saw that her eyes were full of tears, though she was smiling. He watched the car until it was out of sight, and then he went indoors.

He took a box up to his room, to finish collecting his things. Mr. Bogle, too, was packing, as far as he knew. They were active in separate parts of the house, cut off from each other. Harry punched holes in a biscuit tin to make a traveling cage for his mice. The hammering sounded loud enough to bring the old house down on them both like a pack of cards.

The machinery arrived safely at the mill with an accompanying gang to unload it. Several men strolled down from the village to watch them at work. The mist was lapping the knees of the hill; marooned on the brink, the mill felt like an outpost. The silent watchers might have been carrying guns. The gang was glad when they had heaved the stuff indoors. They sat together, drinking tea and pitying the Alsatian which they would not have unchained for the world.

A couple of engineers turned up then, followed by Rupert, and the complicated business of connecting the parts began. The gang pocketed their tips and started off on the long drive back to the factory. The fields on both sides of the road had a layer of mist, and patches of denser fog drifted confusingly across country. Nothing else moved out there; not a dog yelped, not a bird cried. All the gulls might have been lost at sea.

The two engineers worked on until dusk. Rupert was a hindrance; he wanted every part explained, yet he was a poor listener because he was on tenterhooks to get back to the farm. The engineers found it difficult to be patient. The three of them left the mill together, after Rupert had loosed the dog and locked up.

"That's that," said Venn. "You've only got to switch on, Mr. Musgrave. Good luck; and good luck for tomorrow. Give our best wishes to your wife."

"Let us know at once if the machines give any trouble. They ought to run like silk. All the best," said Lowrie, his mate.

Rupert smiled and thanked them, and shook hands. He jumped into his sports car. As he roared up the hill, he remembered he had promised Margaret to collect her prayer book from church. So he stopped in the square, and pushing through the lych-gate, ran hastily up the path. He thought the building might be locked, but it was not. The great door creaked open, like the yawn of a very old giant.

It was already night inside. He was reaching for the switch when a voice called sharply from the far end: "Don't you touch them lights, man!" and next instant the altar sprang up, brilliantly illuminated. Rupert blinked. He spotted Welsh, crouching with a lamp in the chancel among the banked white flowers; he frowned, and walked swiftly up the nave. "What are you doing there?"

Welsh knew how guilty he looked, and his voice was propitiating. "It's just a little favor I promised Vicar. He wanted a microphone rigged up for the Christmas."

"What were you doing in the dark?"

Welsh did not answer at once. Rupert was aware, in the silence, of tiny noises in the space around them, infinitesimal creakings, shiftings, as if the church were alive and breathing. When Welsh spoke his voice sounded loud, though his tone was confidential.

"To tell you the truth that old tramp has been driving me mad. When I heard you coming I thought it was him. I thought, if he sees the light, he'll be in again; that's why I switched it off."

Rupert found Margaret's book on top of the organ, and turned to go. "Have a good Christmas," he said over his shoulder. "Perhaps we'll see you here in the morning."

"Don't you worry!" Welsh cried cheerily from his nest of flowers. "Don't you bother your head anymore, Mr. Musgrave! Believe me, this time tomorrow you'll have nothing to worry about!"

Rupert's heart suddenly lifted, as if Welsh, whom he had never liked, was the one guest he longed for at his wedding. On an impulse he leapt the communion rail and, striding up the chancel, gripped him by the hand. The little man looked taken aback, but he shook hands vigorously, smiling his ratty smile.

"That's nice to know," said Rupert with pleasure. "That's all I wanted to hear. Thanks, Welsh!"

He hurried away, pursued by Welsh's alibi of a smile. Welsh's hands were feeling for the interrupted wiring before Rupert had left the church.

Rupert drove recklessly back to his farm, alight with love and joy.

Venn and Lowrie set off with caution. The shadowy land was on the move, it seemed. Sometimes their road was cut short by a wall of fog, or thronged with separated puffs like new and anxious ghosts. They had to feel their way across the obliterated country.

They had gone about eight miles when they came abruptly on the truck, slewed round and completely blocking the way with its front wheels established in the ditch. Venn got out with a flashlight, and clambered up to peer into the cab. It was empty. He called, "Hallo!" into the fog. No one answered. He guessed that the gang had walked the few miles to the nearest main road where they would try for a lift to a garage. If they could not get help they would go on home, rather than risk being stranded over the Christmas holiday. He guided Lowrie from behind until it was possible to turn the car; they had to drive back to Cormundy.

They parked at the Nag's Head. Mat Shrewberry was drawing beer; he nodded briefly at the strangers.

Venn bought a couple of pints, got change and went out to telephone. He came back after a while, scratching his head.

"Everything's shut. There aren't many garages in the district, and I've tried the lot."

"The Christmas flipping spirit!" said Lowrie gloomily. He turned to Mat. "How do we get onto the highway? There's a ditched truck across the road lower down."

Everyone in the bar moved forward a step, ears pricked for news of an accident. Mat dipped his finger in a puddle of beer and drew a map on the counter. His audience watched critically, and soon began to argue. Venn drained his glass and set it down with a bang. "How far out of our way would you call that?" he demanded.

"Ten miles maybe; not more than fifteen," said Mat. Several voices disputed it. Lowrie looked round and shrugged.

"This is a crummy, out-of-the-way dump to get away from! What do you drive around here, a coach-and-four? You want to move with the times." He followed Venn out.

"We are, you wait!" Rackstraw shouted after them. "You'll read about it in the papers!"

It was now quite dark, and their hearts sank at the delay. The car felt like an icebox. After a few yards they had to stop again, and once more Venn got out with the flashlight. Both front tires had been slashed.

They pulled off the road at the mill gates, and sat and cursed in the dark. Finally they got out of the car, locked it, and climbed wearily back to the pub.

"We want rooms for the night," Venn said in the voice of one at the end of his tether.

"Sorry," said Mat, rubbing up glasses. "We can't put up anyone tonight."

"My —, you'd — better! I'd like to know what — slashed my — tires, that's all!" exclaimed Lowrie in a passion.

Mat looked at them both, and uneasily round the bar. He went out to consult with his wife.

Now Venn and Lowrie were pointedly ignored. They began to feel a little uneasy in their corner. There was a sense of rising excitement, of recklessness in the bar, not related to the rounds of drinks, for it already touched the faces of newcomers pushing their way into the crowd. The center of attraction seemed to be a smiling young man with a look of being slightly wrong in the head. It might have been his birthday, from the number of beers that were bought for him. Whenever he said anything, it was greeted with cheers and jokes, so that he smiled more than ever; but he spoke less as time went on.

Mat reappeared. "You keep your Christmas early," said Venn, turning his back on the company.

"She'll see to it," said Mat to the room at large, ringing up the money left on the counter by people who had helped themselves.

"Listen to me, landlord," said Lowrie. "There must be a policeman, even in this village, and I want to make a report."

"Peter's dry, another for Peter!" someone shouted from the crowd. Mat drew a pint, staring into the foaming brown.

"The constable's away tonight. He won't be back before morning. But if he *was* here," he went on, scrupulously wiping the mug, and standing it squarely on the counter, "he'd be in here, with us."

"Come off it," said Lowrie angrily. "Slashing tires is a criminal offense. The law is the law, even among friends."

"Kids," said Mat. "You know what kids are, these days. How are you going to prove which of them did it? You write out your report, and hand it in in the morning. That's the best thing you can do. I should think," he suggested with a sidelong glance, "you'll be glad of an early night. You'll have to put up with the room, it's all we've got."

Somebody started a song. At once a rival tune was struck up, and everyone joined in one or the other; the red-faced singers roared in their efforts to win the floor. Peter Quotter was being hoisted onto a chair, with a dozen arms to keep him there; he wobbled, but continued to smile. The jollity of the company was aggressive. Venn and Lowrie felt at bay, and when Mat's wife poked her head in at the door to say she had cooked them a bit of supper, they were glad of the excuse to leave the bar. But the noise followed them to the kitchen where they ate, and upstairs when they went to bed. The building rocked with celebrations.

Their room was very poor. They were staring round in dismay, wondering how the two of them were going to fit into the bed, when without any warning Mat came in. He was disconcerted to find them already upstairs. He mumbled an apology and stood on tiptoe, feeling about on top of the wardrobe.

"What do you want, the box? Here, let me," said Lowrie, who was taller, and he lifted it down. But it was lighter than he expected, and tipped over, toppling the contents onto the floor. Mat scrabbled them up. He was scarlet with confusion.

"What's that, your Father Christmas outfit?" asked Venn from the bed where he was sitting to take off his shoes.

"First Father Christmas I've seen with a horse's head," said Lowrie.

Mat stuffed it into the box and went hastily from the room, muttering, "It doesn't belong to me. I've been keeping it for a friend."

Lowrie stepped to the window and raised the curtain. An icy draft was rattling the frame. The church tower loomed within a stone's throw; as he stared at it, the clock began to strike. He sighed and, taking out his diary, sat at the washstand to draft his report. The washstand had a hole in it for a basin, which was missing.

"That clock'll do the quarters," Venn prophesied in a voice of doom. "You can bet your boots it'll do the quarters!"

Harry's room felt stark in its state of unwonted tidiness, with the family faces gone from the walls. He had tied up his books and drawing things, and left himself nothing to do. Mr. Bogle was passing the time by playing his violin; its strains reached Harry every now and then, with a varying acoustic, as if he was strolling from room to room in his favorite troubadour manner. But he kept to his end of the house. Harry sat down by the fire. The fog pushed against his window like urgent breath.

At last he got so hungry, he roused himself to go down and look for some supper. As he turned the corner into the main upstairs passage, he came face to face with a man. They were the same height; Harry's startled gray eyes looked straight into his black ones, as both pulled up with a jerk. The man paused, then backed away smoothly and silently until he disappeared onto the landing.

Harry recognized him at once. He was the *Galantie Showe* man, and the man with the rabbit-skin belt who had been leaping by the bonfire.

It took him a few minutes to recover. He could not get over the horror that the two of them had nearly bumped into each other.

When he reached the hall, he could hear Mr. Bogle's

voice raised in jolly talk in the schoolroom where they ate meals. He went in.

The *Galantie Showe* man was slouching in Harry's chair. He had been eating Harry's supper, but he had paused to pick his teeth with a dessert fork. Mr. Bogle interrupted his discourse, to gauge Harry's reaction.

"Aha!" he then exclaimed. "Meet young Harry Longshaw, the son and heir, the last hope of the line! And this is my very good friend, Dan Quick. What luck for you both to get acquainted!"

Harry went to the sideboard and cut himself bread and cheese. He was famished.

"You'll join us, I hope," said Mr. Bogle. "Quick, a chair."

Quick was concentrating on scraping the last mustard from the pot with the point of his knife. His black eyes did not flicker.

"A rough diamond," Mr. Bogle told Harry in a stagey aside. "But a first-rate, capital fellow. Perhaps you wouldn't mind, yourself—"

Harry pulled up a chair to the table. Dan Quick was the last person he would have expected to be Mr. Bogle's friend. His manners were atrocious, and he smelt strongly of ferret. His hair grew down to his collar and, emerging again thickly at his cuffs, petered out at last on the backs of his fingers. He had an uncomfortable way of sitting, as if he was not accustomed to a chair.

Mr. Bogle had a cache of wine under the table. It

did not take the two of them long to finish a bottle, for though Bogle was abstemious himself, Quick gulped it down like a drain, between voracious attacks upon the supper.

"I met an old friend of yours the other day," Mr. Bogle told Harry . He leant back in his chair, resting his hands on his paunch and revolving his thumbs. "The Honorable Tibby Hopkins. We had a look at his eggs."

Harry was nonplused. He glanced in embarrassment at Quick.

"Three rooms full," Mr. Bogle went on conversationally. "He's added to them since you were last there. We had a long talk about you."

Harry did not know what to say. His cheeks were flaming.

"If you chose to waste your time, that was up to you," said Mr. Bogle in the same light tone. "I haven't used force, not on any of you. You might remember that."

The imperious Quick gestured across the table. Mr. Bogle cagily produced another bottle. Quick wrenched off the cap with his teeth, and took the chance to wet his lips before he filled his glass. He put his hand in his pocket and pulled out a grimy pack of cards.

"We might have come to terms," said Mr. Bogle. "You've had opportunities. Oh, I could have taught you—but you made it clear from the start that you found me ridiculous."

Harry was physically incapable of making a dignified exit, so he stayed where he was. His expression was scornful, though his cheeks were still red. Quick began laying out a patience, matching the cards with lightning speed. He pushed back the used dishes and cutlery as he needed space; a plate, teetering on the edge of the table, fell to the ground with a crash. Mr. Bogle took another biscuit. The front of his cat-skin gown was spattered with crumbs.

The two of them started to play brag. The game began good-humoredly enough, though Quick had a sulky manner that could break up the party, and warned Mr. Bogle not to win too often.

"Oh, I'm no match for my friend," he sighed, losing the kitty for the third time.

"He cheats," said Harry in the cause of justice.

"Of course he does," said Mr. Bogle. "We all do. That's the whole point of a game—to find out *who cheats best*."

Quick said nothing, but he aimed a kick in Harry's direction. Harry looked down. What he saw turned him as white as the cloth. At some point during supper the loathsome Quick had taken off his shoes. He wore no socks, *and his hairy foot was cleft, with two horny toes.*

Mr. Bogle noticed Harry's dismay, and gave a light laugh. "Think nothing of it, dear boy! Old families, as you know, suffer from these trifling aberrations!"

Harry got up and pushed back his chair. He limped

out of the room. He could feel the black eyes of Quick on him to the door, the measuring eyes of a beast of prey.

There was only one telephone, in the hall. He crouched at the bottom of the stairs, his hand shaking so that he could not keep the receiver firmly to his ear. He had to wait before anyone answered, and every moment he expected the schoolroom door to open. The ringing of the telephone seemed to go on for hours. At last it clicked, and he said, "This is Harry."

"Harry? Is anything wrong?" The sound of Margaret's voice, matter-of-fact, rather abrupt, brought him to his senses, as if she had come in while he was having a nightmare and pulled back the curtains.

"It's the Bogle," he said softly. "He's brought in a vile friend."

"What do you mean? What's happened?" She sounded fussed.

Harry paused. He had the feeling that the house was full, crammed with listeners. The very wallpaper seemed to be holding its breath. And in that moment's silence he heard Mr. Bogle's violin, two or three notes from the schoolroom in a flourish, underlining Margaret's words. He went on in an urgent whisper, "He's got a friend in to supper. They're behaving as if they owned the place."

Mr. Bogle struck two gay chords.

"Is his friend called Dan Quick?" Margaret asked, somewhat irritably.

"Yes, how on earth did you know?" The invisible violin quavered in a trill.

"He's the one that's interested in buying the house. Oh, I'm certain I told you about it! Do try to be helpful. You might show him around, and point out any advantages you can think of. Look, if that's all, I must go. I'll see you tomorrow. 'Bye."

The violin sang out in triumph.

Harry put down the receiver, and went up to his room. He could hear Mr. Bogle laughing and chuckling in the schoolroom, as if a prize joke had come his way and he couldn't get over it.

8

Harry switched on both lamps in his room, but all the lamps in the world could not have cheered his thoughts.

He took his mice from the dollhouse and, lying on his bed, let them run about. Happily unaware of their humble status, they explored him with confidence. While he was watching them, he fell asleep.

He dreamt he was alone in the dark. But there was a low murmur of conversation somewhere near, and he moved forward to hear. At once he brushed against a thickness, a shapeless softness dividing him from the speakers. It muffled their voices, though they were very close.

He thought he was ill again, cut off by fever from friends he knew were near, but with whom he could not make any contact. He searched desperately with his hands for a way through the barrier. All the time the unintelligible voices buzzed louder, crushing him with a sense of his own loneliness and confusion; until suddenly it struck him that these invisible companions were enemies. He froze with fear then, in his dream. He tried to run, hobbling off as fast as he could, not knowing in the dark which way to take, only dreading now lest the thickness should separate and release a terrible pursuit. At last he woke up with a jerk. He was out of breath, and very cold and stiff from lying out on top of the covers.

Mr. Bogle was in the room, bending over the grate with his back to Harry. The fire was burning so brightly, EXORIARE ALIQUIS NOSTRIS EX OSSIBUS ULTOR could be read like a motto or speech balloon above him. He turned his head slightly and peered at Harry over the rim of his spectacles. When he saw that he was awake he crossed swiftly to the bed, all friendliness and apology.

"Now the last thing I wanted was to disturb you! I'm afraid I've been taking advantage of your fire to burn my paper toys. I always try to tidy up behind me."

"Where's Dan Quick?" asked Harry sleepily.

"Oh, he left long ago," said Mr. Bogle in a soft voice. He pulled a loose blanket over Harry. "You go back to sleep. Nighty-night." He tiptoed from the room, turning off the lights as he went and closing the door.

Harry shut his eyes. The pull of sleep was irresistible. He was nearly under again, when he remembered the mice.

He felt himself, and the bed around him. They had escaped. He reached for the bedside lamp and pushed the switch, but nothing happened. It must need a new bulb. He was fully awake by this time, and he got off the bed to turn on the other light.

It did not work either. There must be a power cut. With his left hand still on the switch, he turned the handle of the door.

The door was locked.

After a moment he tried the handle again. He felt for the key which he kept on his side; it was not there.

He did not hammer on the door, or shout for Mr. Bogle. He imagined him lurking nearby to enjoy the joke, and he did not want to give him any extra satisfaction.

He went to the fire, and saw at once that there were no more logs in the basket. Mr. Bogle's rubbish, reduced to ashes, littered the grate. He picked out a scorched fragment. It was one of the paper models, the church spire in fact. He squatted there, holding it in trembling fingers, in the flickering firelight.

Then he heard Mr. Bogle's violin in a distant part of the house. He got up at once and moved to the door. The tune was approaching steadily, swelling abruptly to full volume as Mr. Bogle turned down the passage. The threshold creaked as he trod on it, the heavy door reverberated with the harsh noise of the fiddle. Harry said, "Mr. Bogle!" There was no response. He knocked. He lost his self-control; shouted, and banged. The music continued imperturbably. After a few minutes it receded, gradually faded quite away. Harry was left with a clear picture of the whimsical fiddler's rapt and smiling expression.

He fetched the poker. He balanced himself on the arm of the chair and battered at the door. It was a single piece of solid oak; he concentrated on the lock. In time it grew too dark to see, though he went on hitting blindly for a while.

Then he crept onto the hearth. His shirt made a soaking lining to his sweater. The silence was complete, but for the frightened ticking of his watch, an occasional fall of ash in the grate.

Harry never doubted that Mr. Bogle had gone off his head, and there was no way of knowing what he would do next. The house twittered with terrors. He crouched in the dark, at the mercy of his imagination, which was worse than any possible Bogle. He cowered, watery with fear.

Time passed, and nothing happened. He wondered if he could get out by the chimney. It was wide enough as far as he could reach, and not too hot. But it smelled very smoky, and probably narrowed farther up. His legs would hamper him, he dreaded being trapped in a flue. He thought of tearing his sheets into strips and letting himself down from the window. Then he remembered that Margaret had taken them with the rest of the bed linen to the farm. There was a sheer drop from the window to the yard twelve feet below. A well-placed gutter might solve the problem, and he crossed the room to look, though even in daylight it would have been dangerous to trust the rusty plumbing clamped to the walls of Fury Wood.

He suddenly imagined that Mr. Bogle's body was against the door, his gloating eye at the keyhole.

He opened the window, and stuck his head into the frosty air. The pigeon was roosting just outside, on the sill. The fog had cleared, though wisps clung in the wood like shadowy foliage. A paler streak divided the stars like a road through a flowery field. Now he saw that although the house was perfectly dark on this side, not all the lights had fused, for a pinkish glow was reflected on the trees toward the front. Perhaps Mr. Bogle was throwing a mammoth party in the trophy room; as Harry thought of it, he heard a crash in the distance as if people were being careless with the furniture.

A terrified whisper reached him from the ground.

"Harry? Are you up there?"

Harry and the whisperer held their breaths for a moment.

"Who's that?" said Harry in a low voice.

"Me. Toby. *What are you doing up there*?"

Tobias' scared voice brought Harry's own undefined fears sharply into focus. It made him answer calmly: "You might come and let me out. I'm locked in."

"I can't get in through the front."

"There's a door on this side." Harry strained farther out, and now he saw his friend hesitating just underneath; he could have spat on his head. Tobias' flashlight made a yellow circle on the door.

"It's locked."

"It's half glass, smash a pane and unbolt it." Harry waited with bated breath. There was a crash and the tinkle of glass, a silence. Then he heard Tobias in the house. He hobbled across and put his ear to the door. He prayed that the key was still in the lock, that he had not damaged it with the poker.

Tobias came down the passage at a shambling run; the key rattled in the lock. At the last second Harry thought of diving out of the way as Tobias burst through. And a dense smoke that had built up in the passage pressed in with him and began to fill the room.

Tobias was frantic to get out of the house. He hauled Harry along, almost tumbling down the narrow back stairs. Once outside he headed for the stable, and there they both collapsed among the sawdust and wood chippings.

"He's set the house on fire," Harry said hoarsely.

"I don't know which of them did it," gasped Tobias. "It might have been any of them. Even Mat. Probably Mat. He's really bitten with this, mad with it. It's something to do with wanting the land back. They all think it belongs to them, and the house should never have been built here."

"What are you talking about?"

"Half the village—you must have heard them coming up through the wood!"

"I didn't hear a thing." But now he listened to the night. It had the throb of a distant tide.

"I thought you were at Rupert's, I'm sure they all did. You don't mean to say *he* locked you in," said Tobias, touching Harry on the arm to assure himself that he really was rescued.

"Yes, he did; the Bogle did."

"We call him Billy Buck." The name, spoken softly, seemed to hang in the woody darkness.

"What if I'd stayed with the rest? You couldn't have got out with your legs." And again Harry felt that fleeting touch on his arm. "It was just a chance I remembered the cart; I thought I might as well drag it clear."

"*You knew* they were coming here to set the house on fire?"

"Not at first," said Tobias, confused. "Nobody told me anything. But they're in a queer mood. We'd better join them, they mightn't like it if they found us here." Harry said nothing. Tobias was torn between his longing to take part in the excitement of tonight, and loyalty to his friend. "There's going to be some kind of rites," he suggested.

"What rites?"

"I don't know; we'll have missed them, I expect," he admitted unhappily.

Harry crept out of shelter. While he was covering the gap between the stable and the house, the upstairs passage sprang alight with a run of flame. Seconds later something caught and began burning with a steady glow. He stopped in his tracks and looked up. The next window was his, and as he watched, the pigeon spread its wings and flapped to the nearest tree. Suddenly he believed that men might run upon him at any moment with blazing brands. He pulled himself hastily behind the house.

It was still cool and dark on that side, though the tide noise was getting louder. As he passed the kitchen, he heard Mr. Bogle's pets trying to get out. The back door was locked, so he smashed a window, and half a dozen swearing cats leapt over him, all claws, and fled into the wood. He stumbled on, helping himself with a hand along the wall, Tobias following close on his heels. When they reached the trophy room they dropped on all fours under the laurels, and peered round the corner.

The middle of the house was blazing. The doorway gaped, and roared like the jaws of hell. Outside, the fire clung at random to window frames, wooden brackets, the ends of joists piercing the stone. A gutter that ran the length of the roof and had been renovated with pitch cut off the smoking slates with a flickering line. And Harry stared, his face a mask, as though this monster in its death throes had no connection with him at all.

The clearing in front of the house was hotly lit, and a crowd of men stood there. It was like a scene in a puppet theater with its false colors, its exaggerated lighting effects; there was the feeling that unseen hands in the wood would manipulate the shadows linking them to the characters, and push them into action. And the waiting men had an air of readiness, as if they expected this to happen.

Then from between the trees came a strange little procession. Mat Shrewberry led, in his hobbyhorse dress. The false silk legs flapped as he trotted out, not hurrying, following the wavy line that ran through the Horn Dance like a crooked spine. After him came Rackstraw, a bearded, sinister figure in old lady's clothes, carrying a parasol. Welsh brought up the rear in Lincoln green. He struck a toy tune on a triangle as they jogged all round the clearing, watched by the crowd who had bunched instinctively like sheep.

Harry caught his breath. Something huge and dark was moving through the fiery hall. The antlers it wore gave an impression of great height. The step was brushed by the hem of its cat-skin gown.

The crowd pressed forward with a confused cry which presently dropped into the rhythm of a chant: "Billy Buck! Billy Buck! Billy Buck!" Tobias gripped Harry, half sobbing, "He came through the flames! They didn't burn him!"

Mr. Bogle paused a moment in the doorway, acknowledging the cheers. He had assumed a grim majesty in the character of their king. People fell back respectfully from his path as he moved to the mounting block in the center of the clearing, accompanied by his dancers. Welsh dipped into a bucket standing near, and passed him a knife and a dead rabbit.

Mr. Bogle had his back to the house, his gown falling from his humped shoulders in a dark swath. The boys caught the intermittent flash of the blade; assorted rabbit parts were thrown to the ground. "It's the rites," moaned Tobias. He yearned to take part. He would have left Harry then, if he could have been sure that the crowd would accept him as a man.

Suddenly Mr. Bogle raised both his arms and called out: "Mine, to the death!" His voice filled the space between the burning house and the wood. The answer, "Yours!" came from every throat. The crowd jostled forward to press their right hands on the stone, twice-reddened with flames and blood. The scene repeated the ferocity of the blaze; it looked like a concourse of demons. But worst of all were the firelit faces turning from the altar, one after another, rapt, lost.

When the last man had been sworn, the altar was cleansed with a flush of water from the pump. Then Mr. Bogle cast off his majesty, and hitching up his gown, pulled out his violin. He struck a gay flourish of gypsy chords to adjust the mood of the assembly before he settled into the old Horn tune. Rackstraw, Welsh, and Mat trotted off, and the crowd followed in twos and threes. Some carried burning brands, which had dropped from the house, to light the road.

The procession was visible in snatches, winding among the trees, and though it had no appearance of haste it covered the ground surprisingly quickly. At its head skipped the agile Bogle, his fiddle fitfully audible in the frosty wood.

Harry tried to move, and was skewered with a cramp. Tobias went to fetch the cart, crashing hastily under the laurels.

The main beams of the house had begun to snap like twigs, tearing great holes in the roof. Through these, smoke gasped like desperate breath, channeling high into the night. Harry crouched, immobilized, trembling and waiting. At last the conservatory crashed with the din of an elephants' tea party, and in a minute the trophy room flickered with unearthly light. He pulled himself up by the sill. Little flames were running up and down the curtains like snakes. The largest of the animal heads was missing, and he knew where Mr. Bogle had found his horns. It occurred to him that Tobias might not come back; irresistibly drawn to Billy Buck, he might change his mind and follow the crowd. He crossed his fingers and said his prayers. His heart lurched with relief when he heard him fighting a way for the cart through the undergrowth.

They took the back lane to the village. Once they were out of the wood they caught glimpses of flaring torches across the fields, following the main road. Harry sat like a zombie, watching Cormundy Hill move darkly toward them. At first his mind refused to tackle the question of what to do next. He could think of nothing but the destroyed house; he was haunted by an idea of Mr. Bogle floating through the gaping walls, poising in mid-air where floors had been, grinning into the downstairs rooms.

Exoriare aliquis nostris ex ossibus ultor—Arise, thou avenger to come, out of my ashes. And Fury Wood had just gone up in smoke.

And then an idea struck him like a smack in the face. The models, the paper models—suddenly he thought he understood their significance.

Mr. Bogle had burnt them all.

If he was right, it was too late to do anything about the mill, which stood on the main Fury road in the very path of the procession. But the church would be next, and they might be able to save it; at any rate they would have time to warn Rupert at the farm. He was shivering with excitement now, as well as cold; he was tense from head to foot, and cursing his useless legs.

The road lay along the churchyard wall, which towered fifteen feet over it at the bottom of the hill. But a few yards farther up it was low enough to scramble over, and Harry reckoned they had a good chance of getting into the church unseen, even if there were people about in the square. If the mill had already been set on fire, there was no sign of a blaze. As far as this part of Cormundy was concerned, it was still an ordinary night, and even as they passed, a woman in her nightgown, with her hair in curlers, crossed an upper window to switch off the light. He wondered if she knew what her husband was up to.

The thought had hardly crossed his mind, when a black shape dropped from the wall and scuffled briefly with Tobias. The cart rolled back until it rammed the house opposite; Tobias lay spread-eagled in the road. The attacker moved swiftly to the cart and pushed it uphill. His breath fell hotly on Harry's neck; he stank of ferret. He was many times stronger than Tobias, and the steep road sped past. Harry knew who he was; his own hands gripping the cart were white at the knuckles.

Mr. Bogle's procession had halted in the square. The wavering torchlight lacked the drama of fire, and the scene remained dominated by the church, rearing at the back in cliffs of darkness. There was the same air of expectancy about the crowd, though it was less orderly than it had been at Fury Wood. A barrel of beer stood in the doorway of the butcher's shop, and after the walk, people were helping themselves liberally; but they felt entitled to stronger excitements. They had pledged themselves to more than free beer.

Mr. Bogle himself was nowhere to be seen, though his dancers were keeping a clear space in front of the lych-gate. Mat was so carried away by this time that he pranced and fidgeted automatically, while Rackstraw beat back the boldest of the followers with his parasol. Harry was wheeled through the crowd. He made one attempt to roll away, and got a slap that made his ears sing. The trousered legs flicked past. Dan Quick stopped at the front with a free view of the lych-gate and churchyard. Harry stared desperately at Mat, but he did not seem to notice the sudden appearance of the cart; he was locked in his fantasy, tossing his head and pawing at the ground. Harry might have been invisible. He felt sick with panic.

It was almost midnight, and very cold in the square. The magic was wearing thin. But Mr. Bogle was adept at gauging the temper of a mob, and as the clock struck the hour, the thin Horn tune sounded near the church. Such was its power, everyone turned; and froze, staring at the graveyard.

Six images were rising from the crypt, floating over the tombstones, looking in the distance like a band of ghosts quitting the earth for their turn in the dance. This was the sort of conjuring trick the crowd expected; but they had hardly time to catch their breath when the men bearing the images came into sight, weaving among the graves. Their paper hats were painted with horns and suns. They danced across and across in a snaky pattern, gradually approaching the gate, and sidling through it at last to line up three on each side with their backs to the wall. Their gaunt straw images, hoisted on poles, rustled slightly in the draft as they overlooked the square.

Behind swept Mr. Bogle, ducking his horns under the arch of the lych-gate with a speedy genuflection, spreading his sable sleeves with a gesture that at once drew and restrained the crowd. And last of all the giant Titmuss advanced with solemnity down the path. He was darkly enveloped in a voluminous gown. Harry was near enough to catch a whiff of mothballs from the cloth; and then he saw that the butcher was carrying a chopper.

There was a movement from the back; somebody was being passed from hand to hand. Harry had an intimate view of the man's legs, his stumbling feet, and recognized Peter Quotter; a final shove marooned him in the space before Mr. Bogle, where he swayed and smiled, casting hopeful glances back to his friends. His coarse hands were on a level with Harry's face.

Welsh and Rackstraw pushed him to his knees, and Titmuss stepped to the left of him. The six bearers began to chant: "Billy Buck! Billy Buck!"

Harry's eyes were popping with horror and astonishment. He looked frantically to the nearest faces, but everyone was gazing at Mr. Bogle; "Billy Buck! Billy Buck!" the chant was swelling. Men at the back of the square had begun to stamp.

The docile Quotter knelt without a struggle, mercifully drunk. Mr. Bogle raised his hands. He called out, "Mine, to the death!"

"Yours!" they all shouted.

"And beyond!"

"Yes, and beyond! Yours forever, Billy!" Men were waving, throwing up their caps to show their loyalty.

The whole square was beside itself.

Mr. Bogle produced the glittering torque. He held it up for the crowd to see, and passed it to the butcher.

Titmuss took it with an exalted expression and tried to put it on. But his neck was too thick; he could not have worn it without strangling himself. Mr. Bogle saw his difficulty and slightly shook his head. The torque was only a formality. The important thing was to strike, now, with the full consent of the crowd. They had pledged their hands in rabbit's blood; human blood would bind their souls.

But Titmuss believed in formalities. It was his right as executioner to wear the torque, and he did not mean to give it up, short of a hand-to-hand struggle, Mr. Bogle had to wait while he grappled with it. He ground his teeth. The pitiable failure of humans to grasp essentials had exasperated him from the beginning.

Titmuss pulled at the ends of the torque to make it wider. It snapped, and he stood there with a bit in each hand, looking stupid.

Dan Quick had been waiting impatiently for the chop. When the torque broke it struck him as a good joke, and he gave a shout of jeering laughter. He was only off his guard for a moment, but that was all Harry needed to yank at the wheels of the cart and precipitate it, and himself, hard against the shins of Titmuss. Harry was yelling "Stop!" without expecting anyone to hear him or obey.

Somebody in the crowd exclaimed, "It's Harry Longshaw!" and the news went back. Somebody else—Tobias—shouted "Heal him!"

The cry was taken up hysterically: "Heal him! Billy Buck, Billy Buck! Heal him!"

Quotter got up and backed unsteadily into the crowd, and no one prevented him. Now the chopper was glinting at Harry like a wicked eye. He heard Mr. Bogle say, "Harry!" in the voice of a starved man spotting a dinner, and he forced himself to raise his eyes, up, up to the gloomy, horn-crowned head. Then he knew what it was to be hated. But he also saw, without any doubt at all, that this thing of names—the Avenger, Cernunnos, Billy Buck or Beelzebub—was a sham. Blackness, complete blackness filled the gaps of mouth and eyes. If he was sacrificed, it would be by the jealous village. Mr. Bogle could only hate; he could not kill anyone.

Tobias had elbowed his way to the front of the crowd. He shouted again, "Heal him!" Harry had a vision of his innocent, eager face, believing in Mr. Bogle; suddenly he minded that more than anything. He shouted back, "He couldn't heal anyone!" And the nape of his neck awaited the chop of the chopper.

Instead, he was seized with pains in his legs, so excruciating that he screamed aloud and fell off the cart. He had no control over his legs which were jerking spasmodically. But through his agony, through the crowd converging on the miracle, looking with awe from himself to Mr. Bogle, he seemed to hear the doctor's voice: "Bingo! A couple of pains, and you're home!" Tobias dropped to his knees. The pains ebbed, and Harry's eyes refocused on a ring of attentive faces.

In a dead silence, he stood up. He was trembling from head to foot, and he knew that he was cured.

A roar burst from the crowd. He was passed from man to man, a living proof; he was cheered and hugged until he was giddy.

Dan Quick nudged Mr. Bogle. His grin was unpleasantly familiar.

"I suggest," said Mr. Bogle, his voice quivering with impotent rage, "that you keep an eye on young Quotter. Enthusiasm may flag, later on." He fitted his fiddle under his chin, and called to the crowd with the Horn tune. There was an eager response. Emotional villagers tried to touch, or even kiss his gown. He pretended not to notice these marks of esteem, though in his kingdom they were obligatory.

The image-bearers led the way out of the square, their pale dolls rocking against the sky. Another barrel of beer was broached, for everyone felt like a swig to celebrate; refreshed, the crowd streamed down the hill. In the confusion it was easy for Harry to drop behind. He was holding onto Tobias, and shrank with him into Mrs. Shrewberry's dark doorway.

"Lend me your flashlight," he whispered. Tobias felt for it, and handed it over. "Now get your bike, and go and fetch Rupert, go like blazes. They'll set fire to the mill next, and we can't stop them; but if you're quick we may be in time to save the church."

Tobias' jaw dropped. "But he healed you!"

"That's a lie. He wants me dead, and you know it!"

"He can't have meant to lock you in." Tobias was looking after the receding crowd, the torches dipping and flaring. The last people were pressing out of the square.

"You get your bike and go for Rupert." Tobias did not move. Harry raised his fist against the door. "If you don't, I'll fetch out your mother!"

"There's no point in going for Rupert, he can't get here," argued Tobias. "What I mean is, some of the boys have put his cars out of action. Not me," he added quickly. And he thought of an excuse. "They got paid."

There was a terrible pause. Tobias glanced once at Harry's white face, and quickly away.

"They got paid—by the Bogle?" Tobias was silent. "You seem to have gone round the bend; and you still want to run after him, don't you? My God, your mother's going to have something to say about this, and so are all the women!"

"Okay, okay! I'm going," said Tobias, pulling away.

"Margaret's got a car. He can use hers, or his parents'."

"I think they did them all." A measure of guilt, as well as real fear of his mother, had fallen on Tobias. He steadied, now the crowd was out of sight.

Harry climbed the wall and ran to the church, dodging behind the tombstones. From the porch he glanced back. He could still hear feet on the road, the whine of the violin. Everyone would assume that he was the most grateful person in the procession.

He did not expect the church to be locked, but the noise the door made scared him. He left it ajar and, switching on Tobias' flashlight, he walked quickly up the nave, looking to right and left for oil in cans, or any sort of kindling. For a moment he was surprised by the quantities of flowers, and then he remembered that it was Christmas Eve, Margaret's wedding day.

He searched the chancel, the spaces between the choir stalls. The silver cross on the altar flashed like gold in the beam of the flashlight. It did not occur to him to look up at the roof; even if he had, he would have missed Welsh's packets like surprise Christmas presents, tucked out of sight in the carving. Harry could find nothing suspicious; he decided to risk turning on the lights, and hunt again.

The smell of freesias hung richly in the air. As he passed the pulpit, he mounted a couple of steps and flashed the light down. There seemed to be a bundle of old clothes lying at the bottom. He thought—oh horror!—they were hiding something. And then they twitched, and rose in the pulpit like a rusty ghost.

Harry almost fell. The tramp began at once to justify himself.

"I haven't done any harm! I've always fancied a nap in here—it's snug. If you wanted to keep me out in the cold, you should have locked up behind you." Then he caught a glimpse of Harry's face. "Wait a bit! You're not the one who was here earlier on."

"Who was that?"

"That little dark chap that used to be a miner. He was working here all afternoon."

"Working?" The tramp said nothing. "Didn't you ask him what he was up to?" Still the tramp did not speak. But he breathed significantly, in an aura of spirits. "It's worth a pound," said Harry.

"He's rewired the church throughout," said the tramp without hesitation.

Harry got him by the arm and hauled him down the steps. He hustled him down the aisle. When he realized what was happening, the old man put up a flimsy resistance.

"I haven't done any harm! What are you turning me out for? Don't you know there's a law against it? You're assaulting me! Young thug!" From the drafty porch he continued to threaten and protest. Harry turned the key in the lock, and rammed the great bolts home.

The flashlight was failing, but it had served its purpose. He ran to the tower where the bellropes were bunched with their furry bullrush ends. He pulled down the nearest, and began to leap and swing.

9

The strokes of the bell, the Victory bell, sang out across country, ringing the frosty air like stones dropped in a pool. The first of them looped Tobias as he scorched up the track to the farm. The ride had cleared his head, snapped his link with the mob, and now he sped to warn Rupert as if it were the most important thing in the world. He leapt off his bike and battered on the farmhouse door; he panted on the step, wiping at his face with a sweaty hand. Lights sprang up. High overhead in the fans of the trees, a newly-established colony of rooks stirred and looked steeply down upon the yard.

The door opened, throwing a beam across. Moments later Rupert was racing upstairs, while Tobias headed for the stable. The paving rang with the noises of surprised horses. Soon, very soon a party of three galloped out of the yard and thudded up the track. The pollard willows flashed past. Cormundy Hill approached, pricking with a rash of lights; only the throbbing, tolling church remained dark.

The village women came to life when the bell started to peal. Those near the square had already looked out, and wondered what the men were doing. It might be one of their meetings; some sort of playacting perhaps. But somebody playing with the bells and disturbing the children was another matter; they began to dress, and to hunt for scarves to tie over their curlers. Many had uneasy memories of Victory night, and the amount of damage that had been done before morning.

The little back room at the Nag's Head rattled like a dry nut when the bell began. The two engineers jumped awake and fell out of bed simultaneously. They stuffed their feet into the wrong pairs of shoes. Venn tried the door. "We're locked in!" he roared.

Lowrie backed, and rushed the door like a bull. It splintered apart. They hurtled downstairs and into the street, making for the mill where the car was. As they passed the butcher's shop, Dan Quick stepped forward. He seemed to want to bar their way. Venn floored him with a blow and pounded on down the hill. A shiny stream of beer trickled into the square.

Round the next corner they ran headlong into Mr. Bogle.

Venn said later that it gave him a funny turn. It felt, he said, like putting your head into a heap of cobwebs.

The bell had been fixed as a signal if things went wrong, and now Mr. Bogle was hurrying back to the church. He had left his followers gathered in front of the mill. Welsh had already got a leg-up over the railings, and heaved a brick through the window. People were making extra torches from rubbish that had been chucked out during the renovations; the scene was well lit, and rang to the heartening cheer of "Billy Buck!"

All the same, the night was not going entirely to plan. Harry's cure had been gall and wormwood to Mr. Bogle; he still felt queasy because of it. And Mat was proving dangerously unreliable. Mr. Bogle could never resist an emotional temperament, but the publican had completely lost his head. Now, instead of passing the sacred brand to Welsh, he was cavorting about with it, and one of the straw images had already gone up in flames. Mr. Bogle was in no mood to parley with Lowrie and Venn. He flung them off, and stormed on up the hill.

They scrambled up and ran on to charge the crowd. Their onslaught was so unexpected that they got in several good punches before anyone thought of resisting. Confused, men hit out blindly, and soon everyone was fighting. The bearers gave the best account of themselves, swinging their poles as cudgels at the expense of the images.

Rackstraw was the first to miss Mr. Bogle. He raised the alarm and led a party back to the square. Dismayed at being left a prisoner in the little concrete yard, Welsh called piteously after his friends. He could hear the dog snapping and snarling inside the mill, and his terror was that it would find the hole he had smashed in the window, and get out and eat him.

The bell boom rocked the square. Every wall was thrumming, every house showed a light. Mr. Bogle was concerned to find Dan Quick *outside* the church, crouching in fact by the beer barrel with his lips to the tap. Quotter was lying on the ground beside him, snoring peacefully. Mr. Bogle gestured angrily to his colleague as he strode across. He forgot to duck under the lych-gate, and his horns caught in the roof; he wrenched them off and flung them down by the path. The tramp bobbed out to meet him. "Let the butcher pass, sir, he has a chopper!" he cried, quivering with excitement.

Titmuss took up his position in the porch, at right angles to the solid oak door. He heaved his great arms, and there sounded the clunk of iron on wood. Mr. Bogle loomed in the entrance like a thundercloud. "There must be a way in from the crypt!" he exclaimed, rounding on Dan Quick.

Quick did not bother to answer, but he punched his friend.

Rackstraw and his party came trotting through the square. But as Titmuss raised the chopper for a second blow, Mr. Bogle caught the sound of horses cantering along the road to Cormundy, with the rhythm of three times three. For him the hoofbeats rang through the centuries, bringing back old persecutions, old pursuits;

and he missed the mousy noises of the wives, screwing up their courage in the passages before they took the plunge into the bellbound village. Mrs. Shrewberry had gone back for the poker.

"It's the boy, sir, only the boy," the tramp was eagerly explaining. "I tried to stop him, but he threw me out. He used force! He's disturbing the peace, that's what he's doing!"

"*Harry*!" exclaimed Mr. Bogle, and for an instant his expression changed from rage to the deepest self-pity. "The thankless brat! But it's all your fault, Dan, you shouldn't have let him out of your sight. Hurry up, my man, hurry up!" he exhorted Titmuss. Returning to Dan Quick, he went on: "You realize that you have probably lost me the village, just as I had it in my grasp. Oh yes, I know that stuff about eternity; but these men are mortal, and a failure is a failure. Try the windows," he urged, stepping neatly out of reach.

Quick darted down the churchyard. The horses were taking the hill. In the square, dark figures were running in all directions. Those who had dressed up for the occasion, and were more deeply committed, hovered nervously in a corner. Some cried: "Billy Buck? What shall we do now, Billy?"

"Come on, man, come on!" Mr. Bogle roared at Titmuss. It would take only an instant, the flick of a switch to explode the church; he longed to go out with fireworks. And at that moment the lock snapped.

But the great bolts held fast. Mr. Bogle gnashed his

teeth. He plunged out of the porch after Quick, scampered over the graves, leapt the wall like a goat, and raced down through people's gardens, crashing through hedges and flower beds and icy ornamental ponds, scattering bell jars and plastic gnomes.

Rackstraw spotted him. "He's running out on us!" he yelled. He dashed off in pursuit, with Mat and the rest; but alas for their hopeful vengeance—it was at this point that the wives burst into the square.

The Musgrave horses wheeled round the corner and drew up, pawing and rolling their eyes. Panting over their necks, Rupert, Margaret, and Tobias stared round with astonishment. They found themselves in the middle of adult tag, as undignified as most grown-up versions of children's games. As they watched, Rackstraw, dressed for some reason as a woman, caught his boot in his skirt and fell headlong at the feet of his lean daughter. Poor Mat, already captured, was being marched away between his wife and mother. His battered costume made old Mrs. Shrewberry furious. She twitched at the dangling silken legs. "Nonsense!" she was snapping. "Child's play! A man of your age ought to know what he's doing!"

The riders dismounted. The square was a mess, littered with straw and broken glass and puddles of beer. Bits of charred wood lay about, and trampled carnival hats; it looked as though the fun was over. But the bell continued to toll, and Titmuss was still banging away on the church door like an automaton.

They hurried up the path. There was a cracked fiddle lying there, and a pair of antlers. Tobias would not have touched them now for the world.

Harry heard Rupert shouting. He let go of the bell, and the silence flooded up like water.

He felt exhausted. He moved to the door, and leant his head against it. Then he heard Margaret's voice on the other side, near his ear. "Harry? Are you in there? Are you all right?"

"Yes, I'm okay." He smiled. "I'm fine," and then he remembered the lights. He said urgently: "Fetch Welsh, and plenty of flashlights. He's fixed the wiring, you must make him tell you." He paused. "Did they burn the mill?"

"Wait a second," said Margaret. "Here comes Welsh, being pulled along by two men; Rupert seems to know who they are. No, the mill is safe. Do let me in. You're sure you're all right?"

Harry pulled back the bolts and opened the door. The flowery church smelt like a wedding bouquet.

The dog found the hole in the window, and the gap where the railings had been forced apart to free Welsh. It trotted up the street, snuffing here and there until it picked up a scent and ran off, away from the village. Before long it had covered a considerable distance.

An old gamekeeper was making his rounds at dawn when he came on some puzzling tracks in the corner of a field. A large dog had been there, that was plain; but there were other prints. He could have called them cows', if cows had ever been known to run in pairs, upright. He stood for several minutes looking down, rubbing his bristly jaw.

He shuffled on, over the crunchy grass. Mouthfuls of tabby fur were lying in the ditch. There were rabbit skins, too, strewn around; he bent stiffly in the rimy, misty field.

"Ruddy poachers," he grumbled, stirring them with his boot.

Format by Kohar Alexanian
Set in 11 pt. Linotype Caslon
Composed, printed and bound by American Book–Stratford Press, Inc.
HARPER & ROW, PUBLISHERS, INCORPORATED